DESTINATION MOON

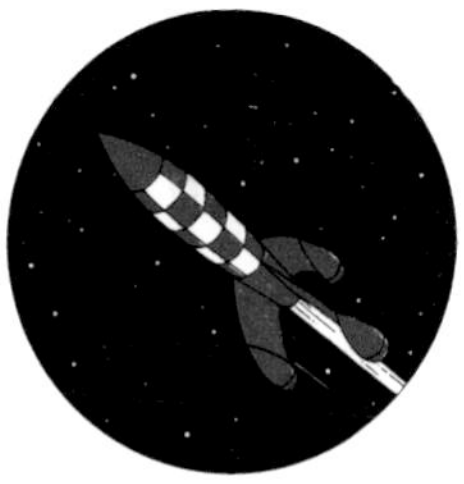

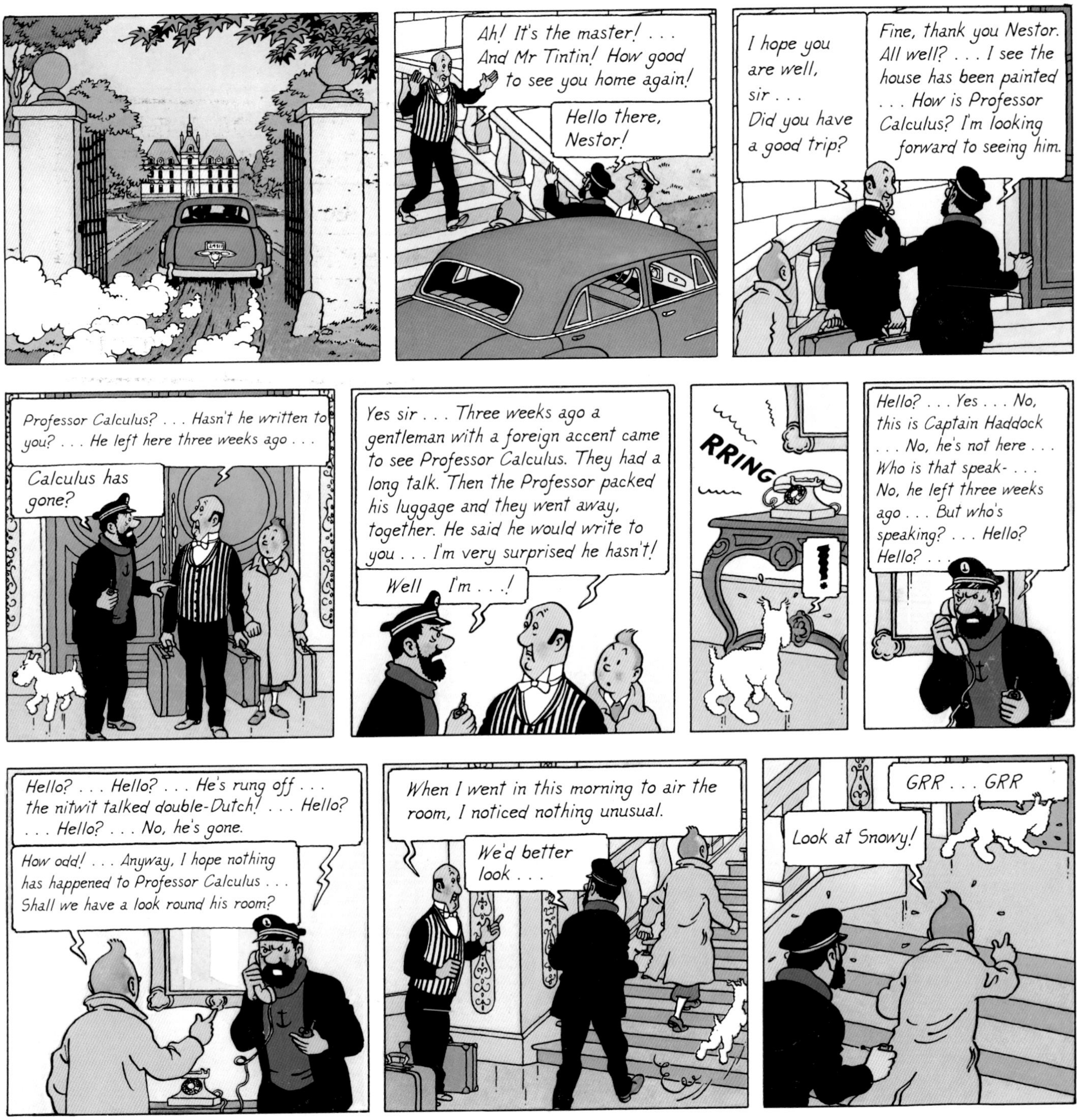
Ah! It's the master! . . . And Mr Tintin! How good to see you home again!
Hello there, Nestor!
I hope you are well, sir . . . Did you have a good trip?
Fine, thank you Nestor. All well? . . . I see the house has been painted . . . How is Professor Calculus? I'm looking forward to seeing him.
Professor Calculus? . . . Hasn't he written to you? . . . He left here three weeks ago . . .
Calculus has gone?
Yes sir . . . Three weeks ago a gentleman with a foreign accent came to see Professor Calculus. They had a long talk. Then the Professor packed his luggage and they went away, together. He said he would write to you . . . I'm very surprised he hasn't!
Well . . . I'm . . .!
RRING
Hello? . . . Yes . . . No, this is Captain Haddock . . . No, he's not here . . . Who is that speak- . . . No, he left three weeks ago . . . But who's speaking? . . . Hello? Hello? . . .
Hello? . . . Hello? . . . He's rung off . . . the nitwit talked double-Dutch! . . . Hello? . . . Hello? . . . No, he's gone.
How odd! . . . Anyway, I hope nothing has happened to Professor Calculus . . . Shall we have a look round his room?
When I went in this morning to air the room, I noticed nothing unusual.
We'd better look . . .
GRR . . . GRR
Look at Snowy!

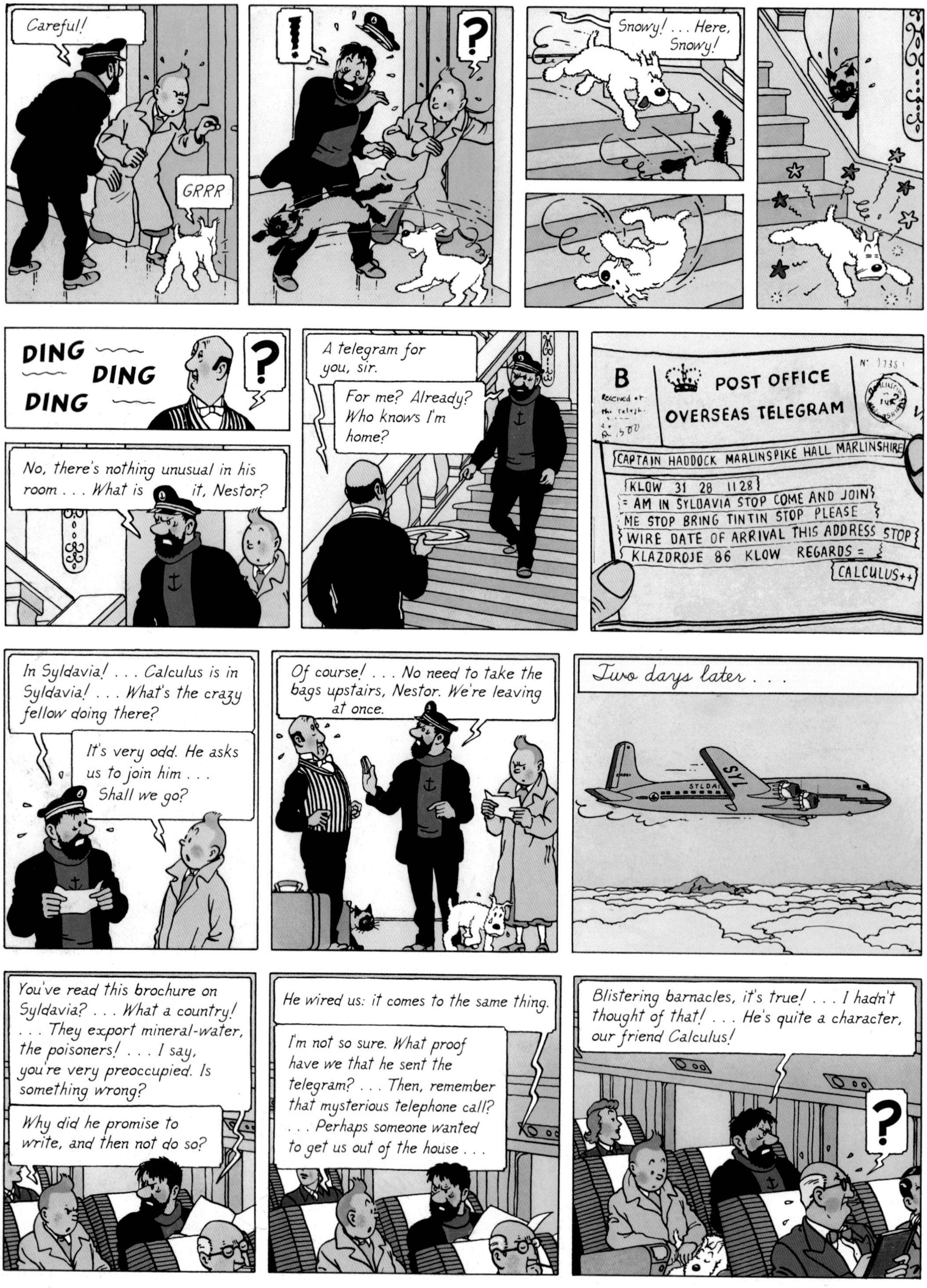
Careful!
GRRR
Snowy! . . . Here, Snowy!
DING DING DING
No, there's nothing unusual in his room . . . What is it, Nestor?
A telegram for you, sir.
For me? Already? Who knows I'm home?
POST OFFICE
OVERSEAS TELEGRAM
CAPTAIN HADDOCK MARLINSPIKE HALL MARLINSHIRE
KLOW 31 28 1128
= AM IN SYLDAVIA STOP COME AND JOIN ME STOP BRING TINTIN STOP PLEASE WIRE DATE OF ARRIVAL THIS ADDRESS STOP KLAZDROJE 86 KLOW REGARDS =
CALCULUS++
In Syldavia! . . . Calculus is in Syldavia! . . . What's the crazy fellow doing there?
It's very odd. He asks us to join him . . . Shall we go?
Of course! . . . No need to take the bags upstairs, Nestor. We're leaving at once.
Two days later . . .
You've read this brochure on Syldavia? . . . What a country! . . . They export mineral-water, the poisoners! . . . I say, you're very preoccupied. Is something wrong?
Why did he promise to write, and then not do so?
He wired us: it comes to the same thing.
I'm not so sure. What proof have we that he sent the telegram? . . . Then, remember that mysterious telephone call? . . . Perhaps someone wanted to get us out of the house . . .
Blistering barnacles, it's true! . . . I hadn't thought of that! . . . He's quite a character, our friend Calculus!

HERGÉ
★
THE ADVENTURES OF
TINTIN
★

DESTINATION MOON

EGMONT

The TINTIN books are published in the following languages:

Alsacien	CASTERMAN
Basque	ELKAR
Bengali	ANANDA
Bernese	EMMENTALER DRUCK
Breton	AN HERE
Catalan	CASTERMAN
Chinese	CASTERMAN/CHINA CHILDREN PUBLISHING
Corsican	CASTERMAN
Danish	CARLSEN
Dutch	CASTERMAN
English	EGMONT UK LTD/LITTLE, BROWN & CO.
Esperanto	ESPERANTIX/CASTERMAN
Finnish	OTAVA
French	CASTERMAN
Gallo	RUE DES SCRIBES
Gaumais	CASTERMAN
German	CARLSEN
Greek	CASTERMAN
Hebrew	MIZRAHI
Indonesian	INDIRA
Italian	CASTERMAN
Japanese	FUKUINKAN
Korean	CASTERMAN/SOL
Latin	ELI/CASTERMAN
Luxembourgeois	IMPRIMERIE SAINT-PAUL
Norwegian	EGMONT
Picard	CASTERMAN
Polish	CASTERMAN/MOTOPOL
Portuguese	CASTERMAN
Provençal	CASTERMAN
Romanche	LIGIA ROMONTSCHA
Russian	CASTERMAN
Serbo-Croatian	DECJE NOVINE
Spanish	CASTERMAN
Swedish	CARLSEN
Thai	CASTERMAN
Tibetan	CASTERMAN
Turkish	YAPI KREDI YAYINLARI

TRANSLATED BY
LESLIE LONSDALE-COOPER AND MICHAEL TURNER

EGMONT
We bring stories to life

Artwork copyright © 1959 by Editions Casterman, Paris and Tournai
Copyright © renewed 1981 by Casterman
Text copyright © 1959 by Egmont UK Limited
First published in Great Britain in 1959 by Methuen Children's Books
Hardback edition published in 2009, paperback edition published in 2012 by
Egmont UK Limited, The Yellow Building, 1 Nicholas Road, London, W11 4AN

Library of Congress Catalogue Card Numbers Afor 12985 and R 10422

Hardback: ISBN 978 1 4052 0815 4
Paperback: ISBN 978 1 4052 0627 3

Printed in China

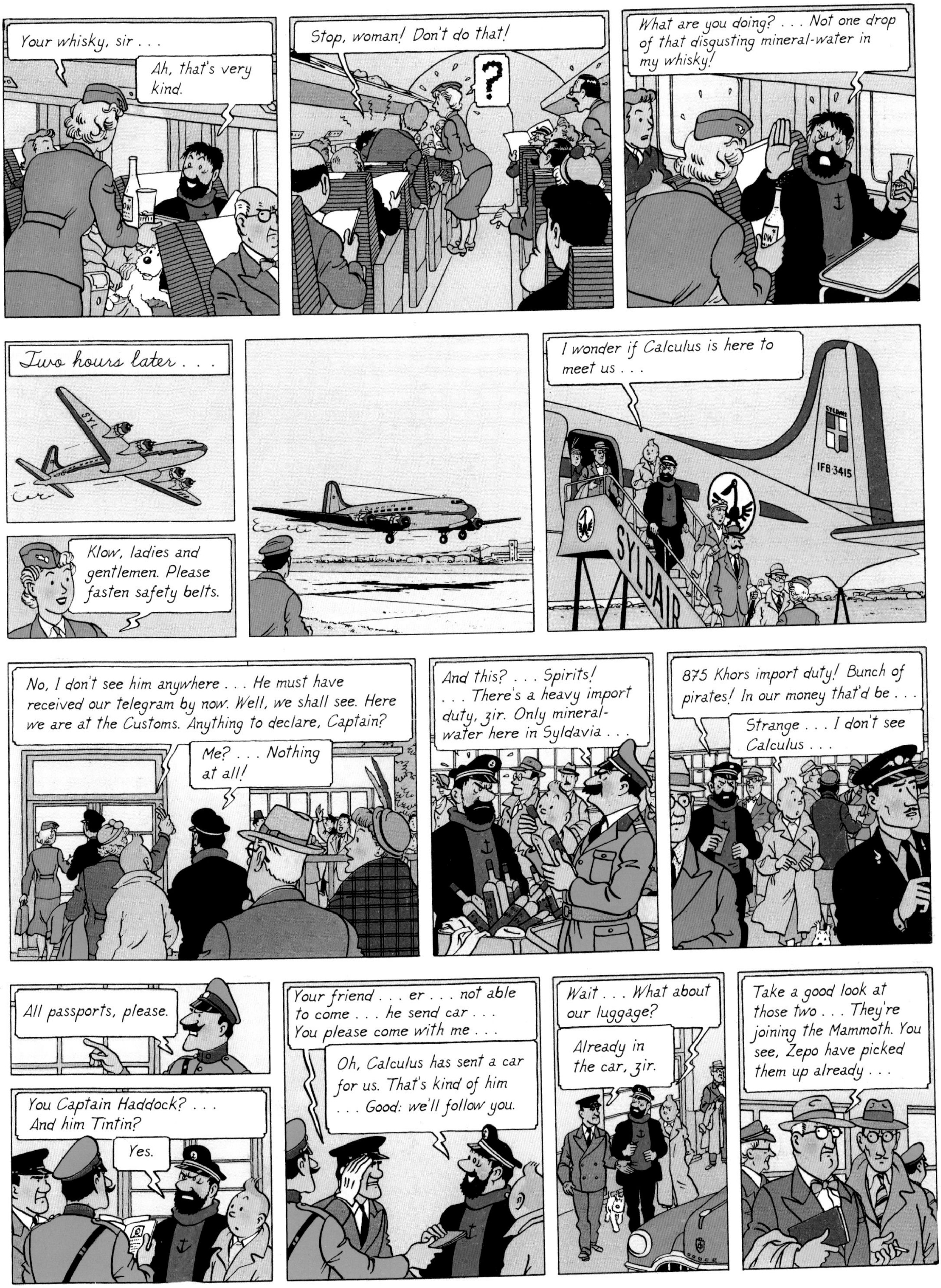
Your whisky, sir . . .
Ah, that's very kind.
Stop, woman! Don't do that!
?
What are you doing? . . . Not one drop of that disgusting mineral-water in my whisky!
Two hours later . . .
Klow, ladies and gentlemen. Please fasten safety belts.
I wonder if Calculus is here to meet us . . .
IFB-3415
SYLDAIR
No, I don't see him anywhere . . . He must have received our telegram by now. Well, we shall see. Here we are at the Customs. Anything to declare, Captain?
Me? . . . Nothing at all!
And this? . . . Spirits! . . . There's a heavy import duty, zir. Only mineral-water here in Syldavia . . .
875 Khors import duty! Bunch of pirates! In our money that'd be . . .
Strange . . . I don't see Calculus . . .
All passports, please.
You Captain Haddock? . . . And him Tintin?
Yes.
Your friend . . . er . . . not able to come . . . he send car . . . You please come with me . . .
Oh, Calculus has sent a car for us. That's kind of him . . . Good: we'll follow you.
Wait . . . What about our luggage?
Already in the car, zir.
Take a good look at those two . . . They're joining the Mammoth. You see, Zepo have picked them up already . . .

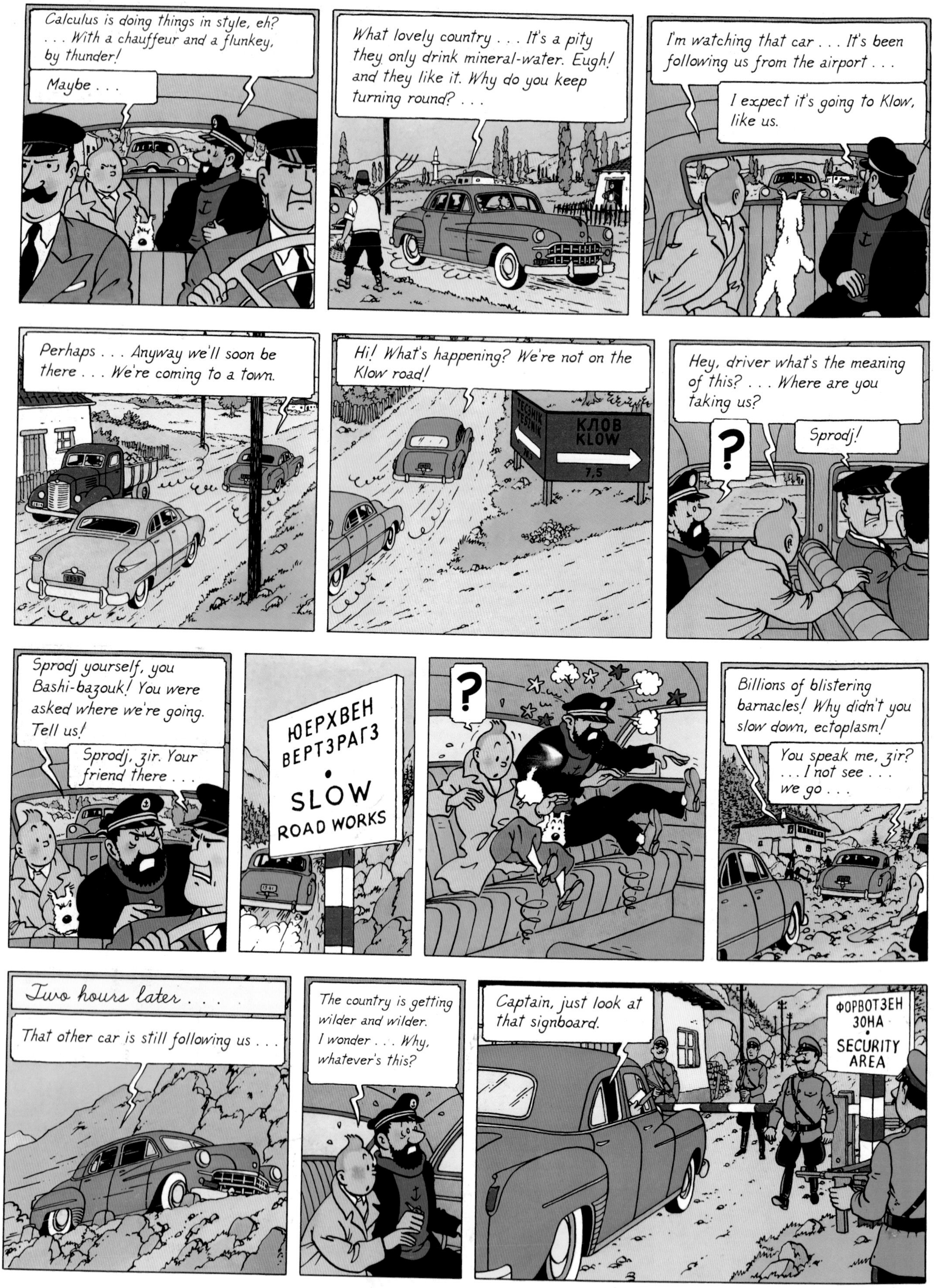

Calculus is doing things in style, eh? . . . With a chauffeur and a flunkey, by thunder!
Maybe . . .
What lovely country . . . It's a pity they only drink mineral-water. Eugh! and they like it. Why do you keep turning round? . . .
I'm watching that car . . . It's been following us from the airport . . .
I expect it's going to Klow, like us.
Perhaps . . . Anyway we'll soon be there . . . We're coming to a town.
Hi! What's happening? We're not on the Klow road!
КЛОВ
KLOW
7,5
Hey, driver what's the meaning of this? . . . Where are you taking us?
?
Sprodj!
Sprodj yourself, you Bashi-bazouk! You were asked where we're going. Tell us!
Sprodj, zir. Your friend there . . .
ЮЕРХВЕН
ВЕРТЗРАГЗ
SLOW
ROAD WORKS
?
Billions of blistering barnacles! Why didn't you slow down, ectoplasm!
You speak me, zir? . . . I not see . . . we go . . .
Two hours later . . .
That other car is still following us . . .
The country is getting wilder and wilder. I wonder . . . Why, whatever's this?
Captain, just look at that signboard.
ФОРВОТЗЕН
ЗОНА
SECURITY
AREA

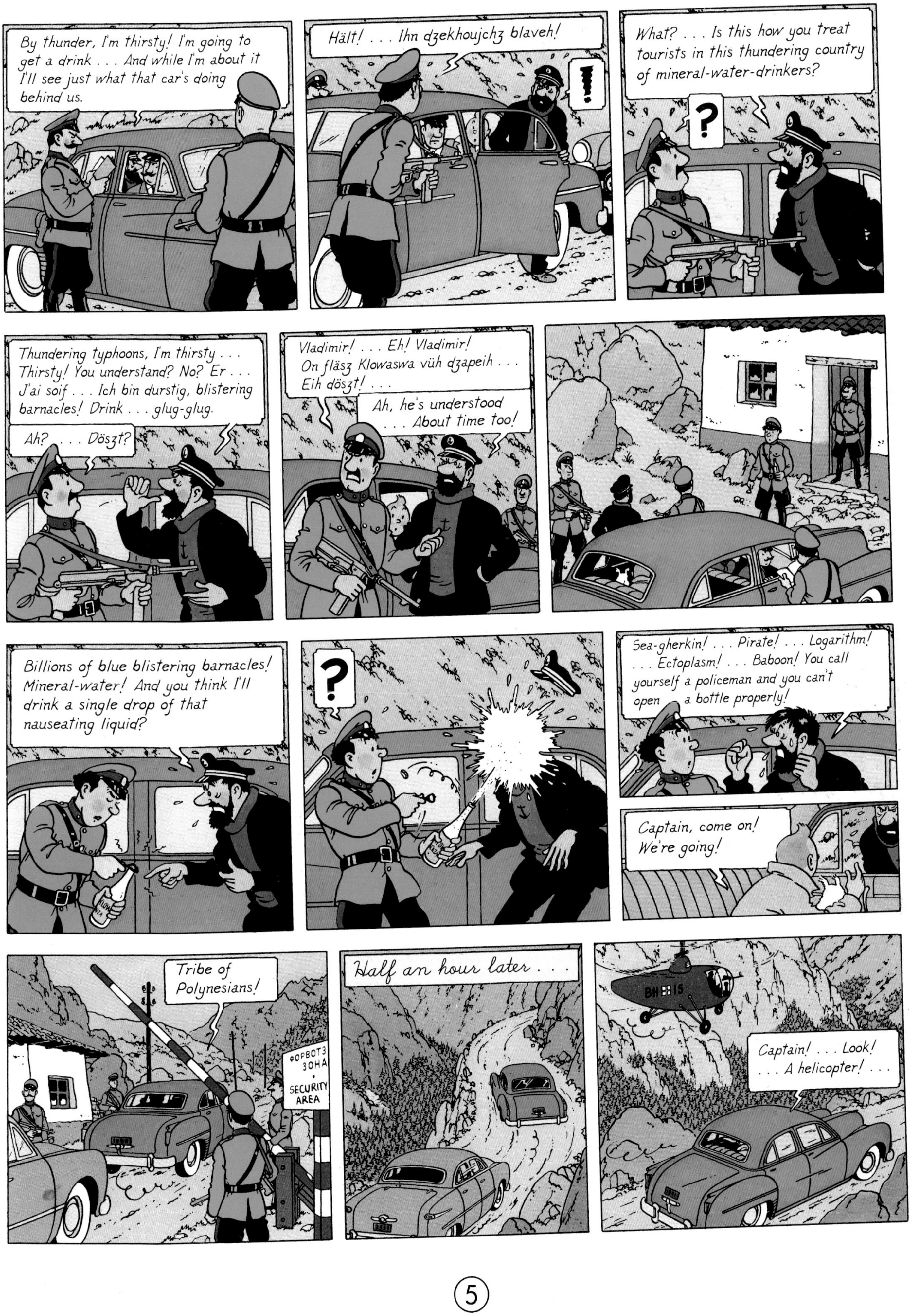
By thunder, I'm thirsty! I'm going to get a drink . . . And while I'm about it I'll see just what that car's doing behind us.
Hält! . . . Ihn dzekhoujchz blaveh!
!
What? . . . Is this how you treat tourists in this thundering country of mineral-water-drinkers?
?
Thundering typhoons, I'm thirsty . . . Thirsty! You understand? No? Er . . . J'ai soif . . . Ich bin durstig, blistering barnacles! Drink . . . glug-glug.
Ah? . . . Döszt?
Vladimir! . . . Eh! Vladimir! On fläsz Klowaswa vüh dzapeih . . . Eih döszt! . . .
Ah, he's understood . . . About time too!
Billions of blue blistering barnacles! Mineral-water! And you think I'll drink a single drop of that nauseating liquid?
?
Sea-gherkin! . . . Pirate! . . . Logarithm! . . . Ectoplasm! . . . Baboon! You call yourself a policeman and you can't open a bottle properly!
Captain, come on! We're going!
Tribe of Polynesians!
ФОРВОТЗ
ЗОНА
SECURITY AREA
Half an hour later . . .
BH 15
Captain! . . . Look! . . . A helicopter! . . .

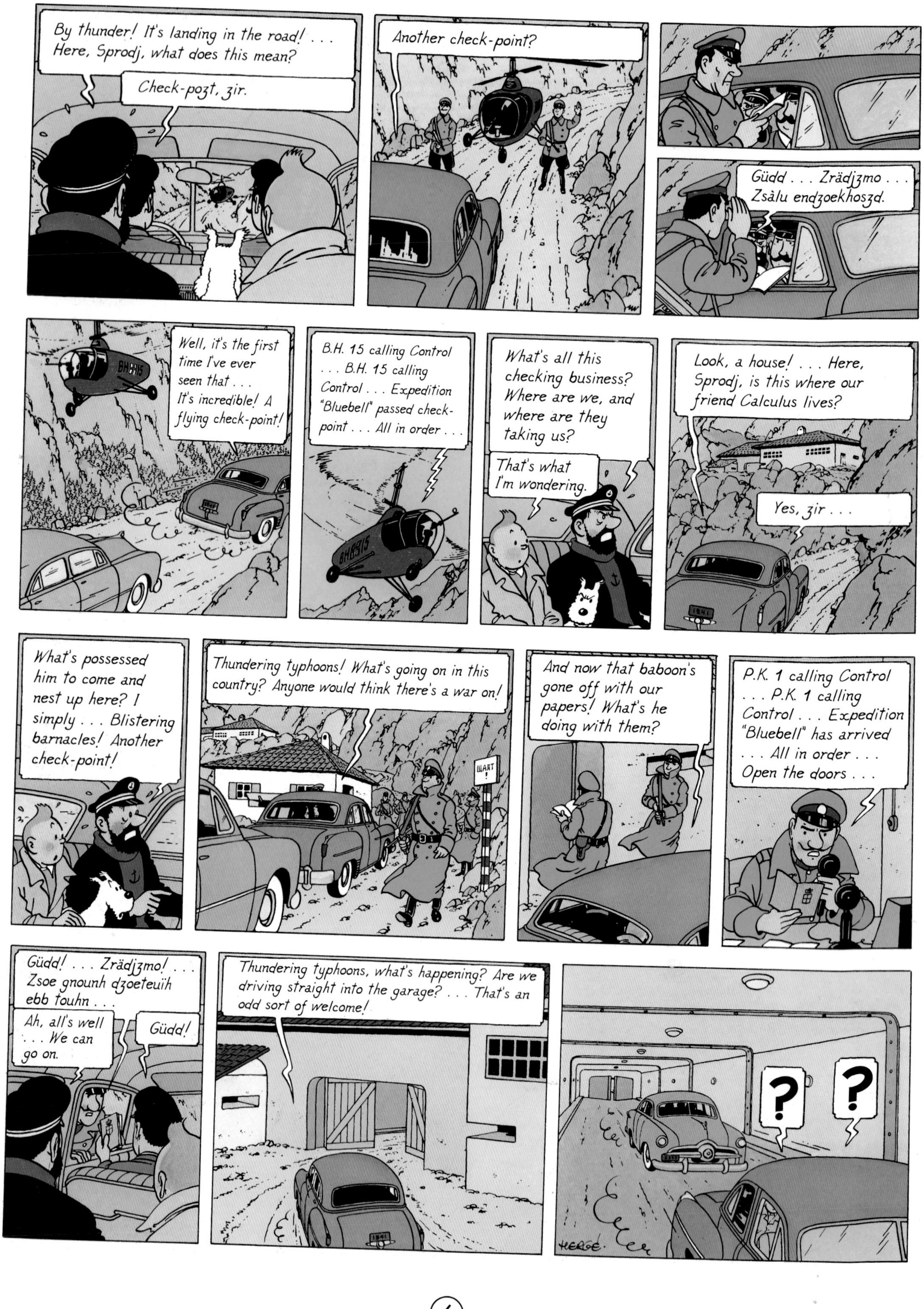
By thunder! It's landing in the road! . . . Here, Sprodj, what does this mean?
Check-pozt, zir.
Another check-point?
Güdd . . . Zrädjzmo . . . Zsàlu endzoekhoszd.
Well, it's the first time I've ever seen that . . . It's incredible! A flying check-point!
B.H. 15 calling Control . . . B.H. 15 calling Control . . . Expedition "Bluebell" passed check-point . . . All in order . . .
What's all this checking business? Where are we, and where are they taking us?
That's what I'm wondering.
Look, a house! . . . Here, Sprodj, is this where our friend Calculus lives?
Yes, zir . . .
What's possessed him to come and nest up here? I simply . . . Blistering barnacles! Another check-point!
Thundering typhoons! What's going on in this country? Anyone would think there's a war on!
And now that baboon's gone off with our papers! What's he doing with them?
P.K. 1 calling Control . . . P.K. 1 calling Control . . . Expedition "Bluebell" has arrived . . . All in order . . . Open the doors . . .
Güdd! . . . Zrädjzmo! . . . Zsoe gnounh dzoeteuïh ebb touhn . . .
Ah, all's well . . . We can go on.
Güdd!
Thundering typhoons, what's happening? Are we driving straight into the garage? . . . That's an odd sort of welcome!
?
?
HERGÉ

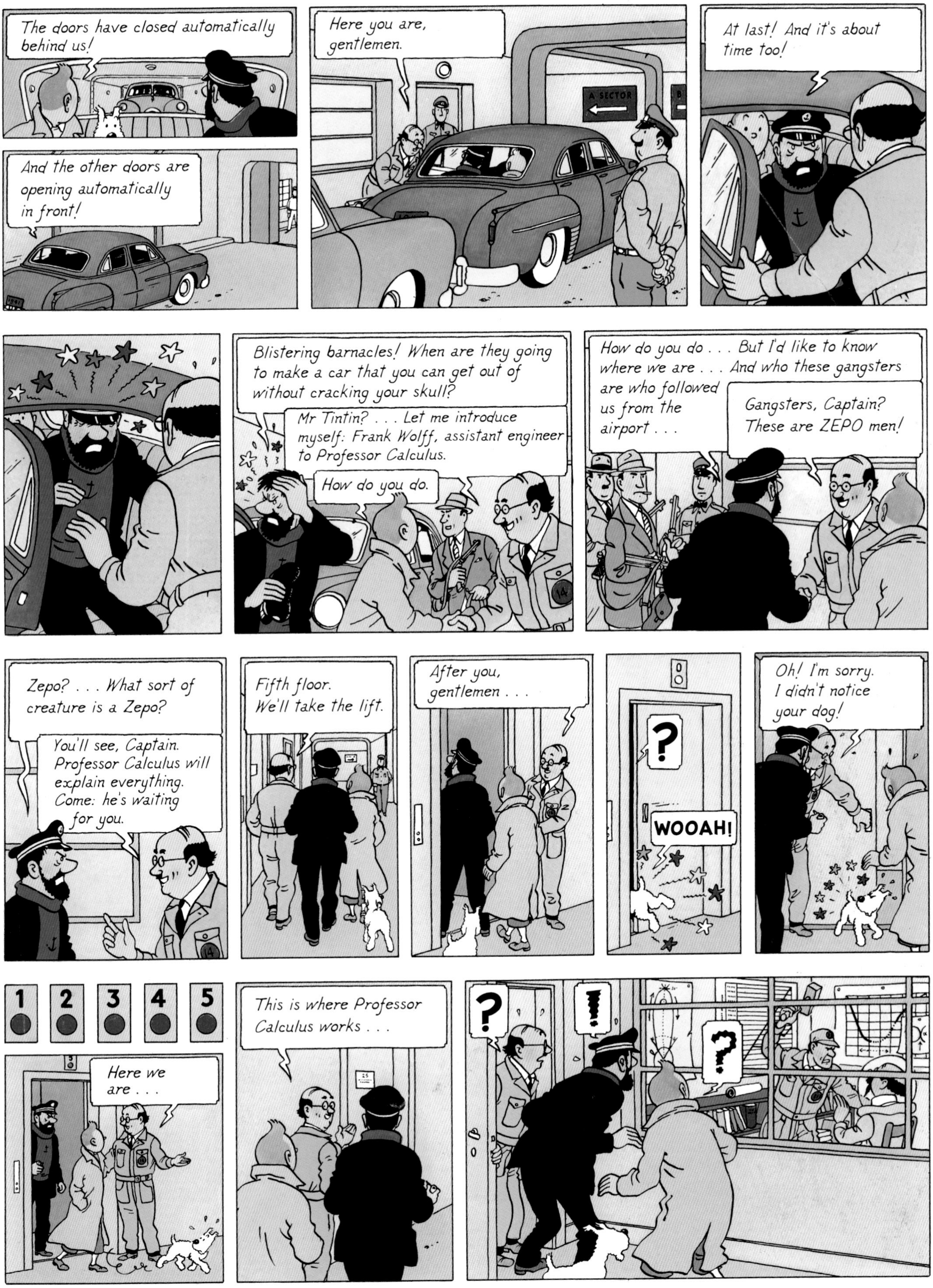
The doors have closed automatically behind us!
And the other doors are opening automatically in front!
Here you are, gentlemen.
A SECTOR
At last! And it's about time too!
Blistering barnacles! When are they going to make a car that you can get out of without cracking your skull?
Mr Tintin? . . . Let me introduce myself: Frank Wolff, assistant engineer to Professor Calculus.
How do you do.
How do you do . . . But I'd like to know where we are . . . And who these gangsters are who followed us from the airport . . .
Gangsters, Captain? These are ZEPO men!
Zepo? . . . What sort of creature is a Zepo?
You'll see, Captain. Professor Calculus will explain everything. Come: he's waiting for you.
Fifth floor. We'll take the lift.
After you, gentlemen . . .
?
WOOAH!
Oh! I'm sorry. I didn't notice your dog!
1
2
3
4
5
Here we are . . .
This is where Professor Calculus works . . .
?
!
?

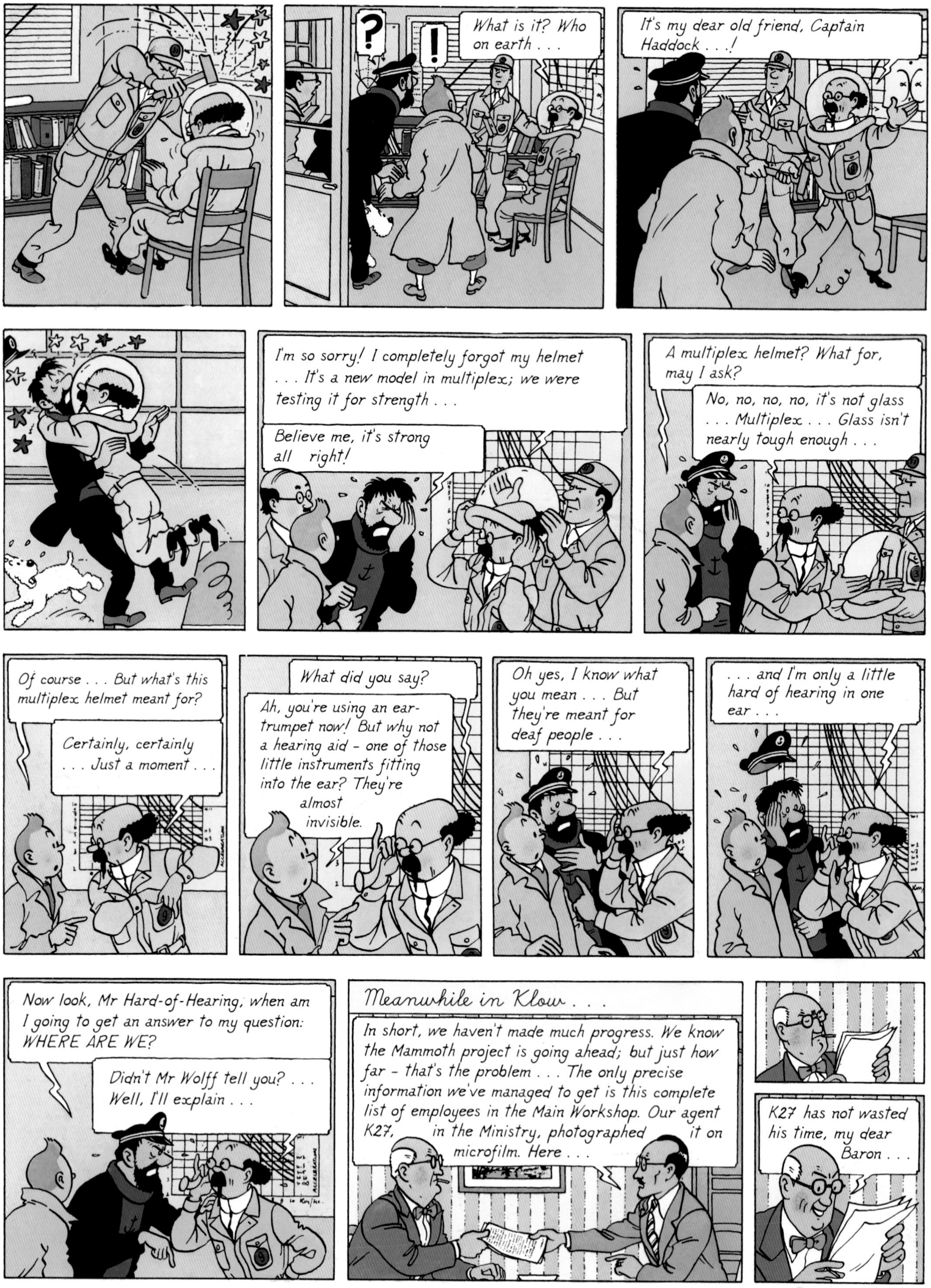
What is it? Who on earth . . .
It's my dear old friend, Captain Haddock . . .!
I'm so sorry! I completely forgot my helmet . . . It's a new model in multiplex; we were testing it for strength . . .
Believe me, it's strong all right!
A multiplex helmet? What for, may I ask?
No, no, no, no, it's not glass . . . Multiplex . . . Glass isn't nearly tough enough . . .
Of course . . . But what's this multiplex helmet meant for?
Certainly, certainly . . . Just a moment . . .
What did you say?
Ah, you're using an ear-trumpet now! But why not a hearing aid - one of those little instruments fitting into the ear? They're almost invisible.
Oh yes, I know what you mean . . . But they're meant for deaf people . . .
. . . and I'm only a little hard of hearing in one ear . . .
Now look, Mr Hard-of-Hearing, when am I going to get an answer to my question: WHERE ARE WE?
Didn't Mr Wolff tell you? . . . Well, I'll explain . . .
Meanwhile in Klow . . .
In short, we haven't made much progress. We know the Mammoth project is going ahead; but just how far - that's the problem . . . The only precise information we've managed to get is this complete list of employees in the Main Workshop. Our agent K27, in the Ministry, photographed it on microfilm. Here . . .
K27 has not wasted his time, my dear Baron . . .

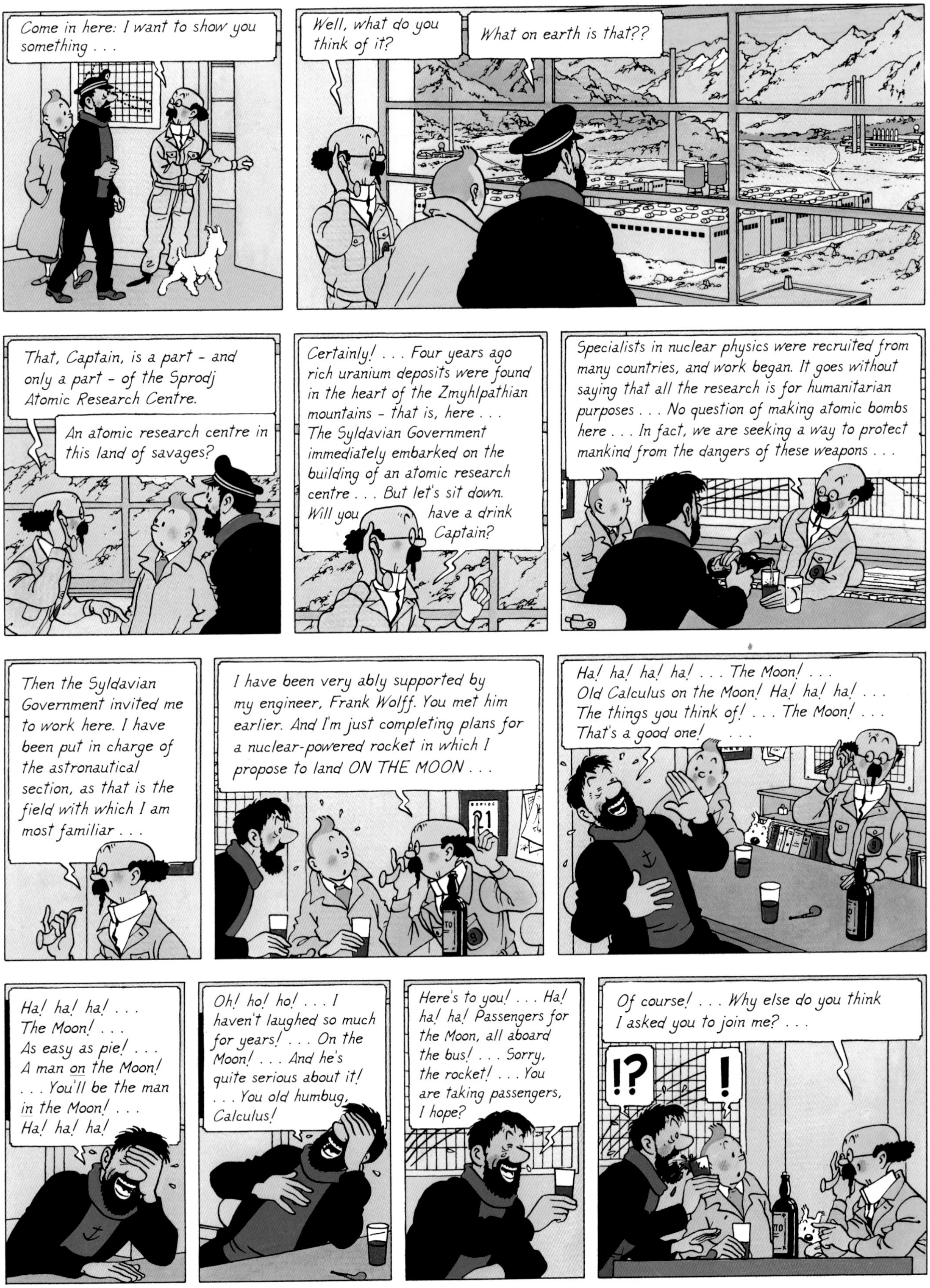

Come in here: I want to show you something . . .
Well, what do you think of it?
What on earth is that??
That, Captain, is a part - and only a part - of the Sprodj Atomic Research Centre.
An atomic research centre in this land of savages?
Certainly! . . . Four years ago rich uranium deposits were found in the heart of the Zmyhlpathian mountains - that is, here . . . The Syldavian Government immediately embarked on the building of an atomic research centre . . . But let's sit down. Will you have a drink Captain?
Specialists in nuclear physics were recruited from many countries, and work began. It goes without saying that all the research is for humanitarian purposes . . . No question of making atomic bombs here . . . In fact, we are seeking a way to protect mankind from the dangers of these weapons . . .
Then the Syldavian Government invited me to work here. I have been put in charge of the astronautical section, as that is the field with which I am most familiar . . .
I have been very ably supported by my engineer, Frank Wolff. You met him earlier. And I'm just completing plans for a nuclear-powered rocket in which I propose to land ON THE MOON . . .
Ha! ha! ha! ha! . . . The Moon! . . . Old Calculus on the Moon! Ha! ha! ha! . . . The things you think of! . . . The Moon! . . . That's a good one! . . .
Ha! ha! ha! . . . The Moon! . . . As easy as pie! . . . A man on the Moon! . . . You'll be the man in the Moon! . . . Ha! ha! ha!
Oh! ho! ho! . . . I haven't laughed so much for years! . . . On the Moon! . . . And he's quite serious about it! . . . You old humbug, Calculus!
Here's to you! . . . Ha! ha! ha! Passengers for the Moon, all aboard the bus! . . . Sorry, the rocket! . . . You are taking passengers, I hope?
Of course! . . . Why else do you think I asked you to join me? . . .
!?
!

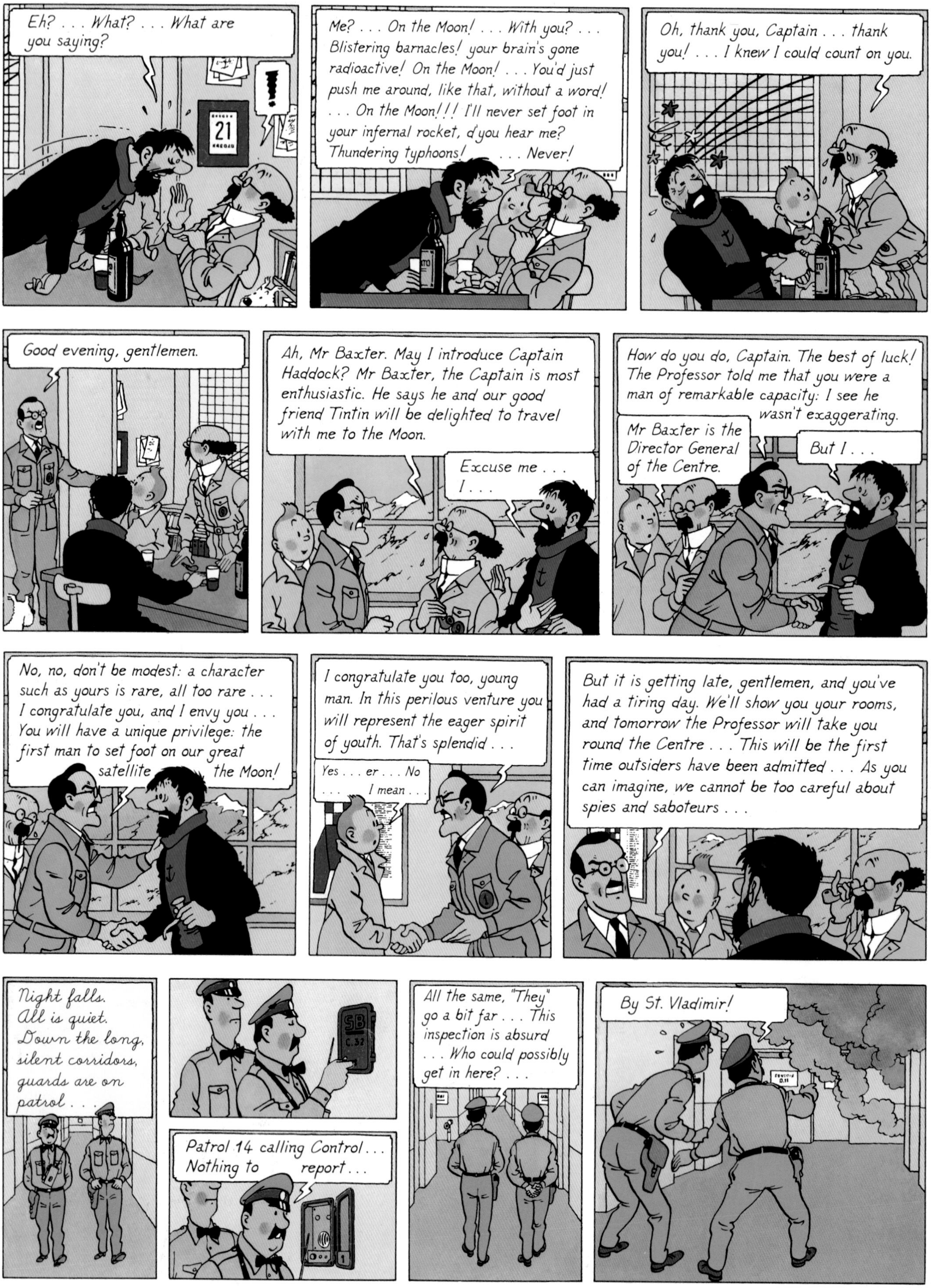

Eh? . . . What? . . . What are you saying?
Me? . . . On the Moon! . . . With you? . . . Blistering barnacles! your brain's gone radioactive! On the Moon! . . . You'd just push me around, like that, without a word! . . . On the Moon!!! I'll never set foot in your infernal rocket, d'you hear me? Thundering typhoons! . . . Never!
Oh, thank you, Captain . . . thank you! . . . I knew I could count on you.
Good evening, gentlemen.
Ah, Mr Baxter. May I introduce Captain Haddock? Mr Baxter, the Captain is most enthusiastic. He says he and our good friend Tintin will be delighted to travel with me to the Moon.
Excuse me . . . I . . .
How do you do, Captain. The best of luck! The Professor told me that you were a man of remarkable capacity: I see he wasn't exaggerating.
Mr Baxter is the Director General of the Centre.
But I . . .
No, no, don't be modest: a character such as yours is rare, all too rare . . . I congratulate you, and I envy you . . . You will have a unique privilege: the first man to set foot on our great satellite the Moon!
I congratulate you too, young man. In this perilous venture you will represent the eager spirit of youth. That's splendid . . .
Yes . . . er . . . No . . . I mean . . .
But it is getting late, gentlemen, and you've had a tiring day. We'll show you your rooms, and tomorrow the Professor will take you round the Centre . . . This will be the first time outsiders have been admitted . . . As you can imagine, we cannot be too careful about spies and saboteurs . . .
Night falls. All is quiet. Down the long, silent corridors, guards are on patrol . . .
Patrol 14 calling Control . . . Nothing to report . . .
All the same, "They" go a bit far . . . This inspection is absurd . . . Who could possibly get in here? . . .
By St. Vladimir!

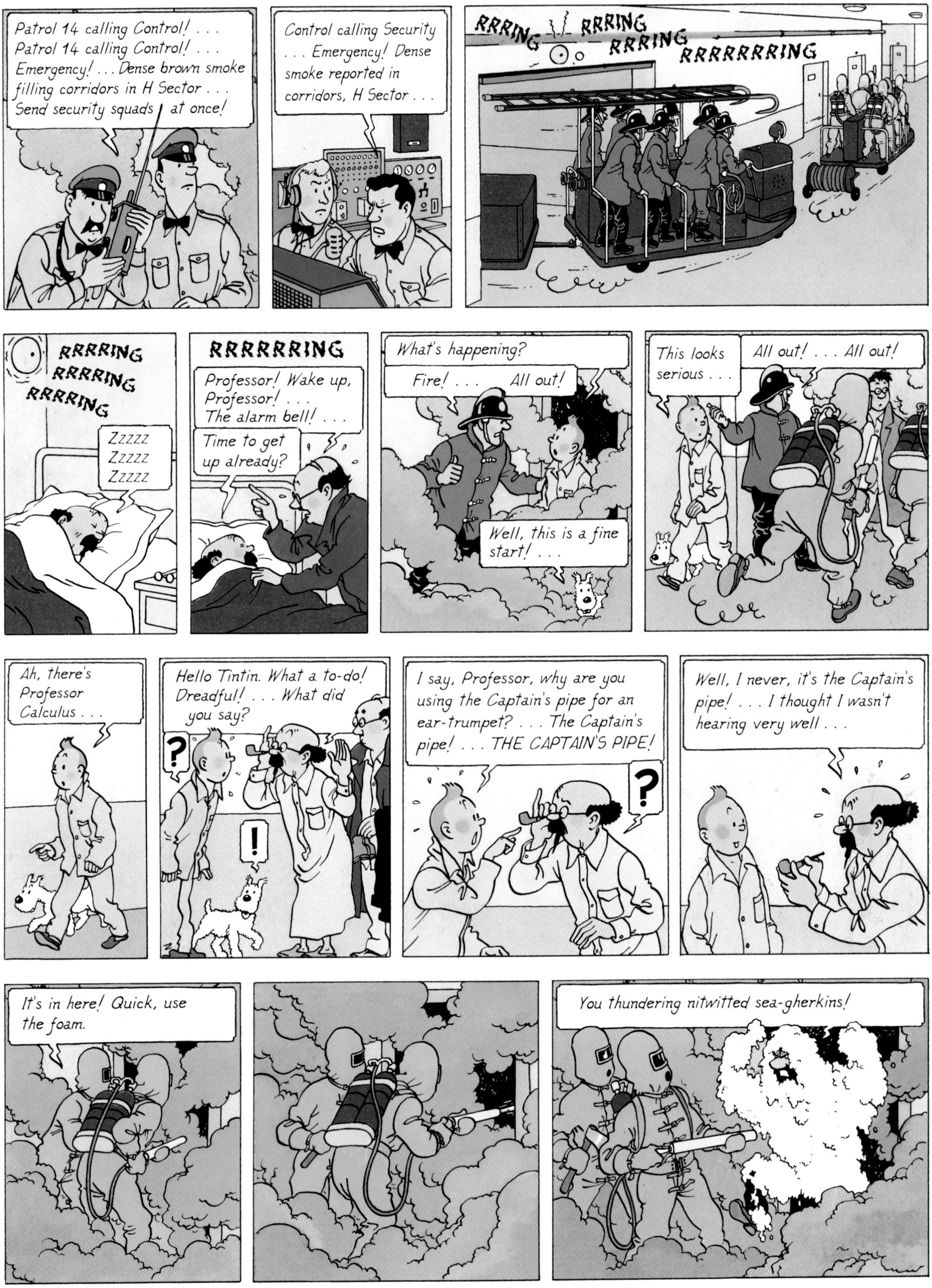

Patrol 14 calling Control! . . . Patrol 14 calling Control! . . . Emergency! . . . Dense brown smoke filling corridors in H Sector . . . Send security squads at once!
Control calling Security . . . Emergency! Dense smoke reported in corridors, H Sector . . .
RRRING RRRING RRRING RRRRRRRRING
RRRRING RRRRING RRRRING
Zzzzz Zzzzz Zzzzz
RRRRRRRING
Professor! Wake up, Professor! . . . The alarm bell! . . .
Time to get up already?
What's happening?
Fire! . . . All out!
Well, this is a fine start! . . .
This looks serious . . .
All out! . . . All out!
Ah, there's Professor Calculus . . .
Hello Tintin. What a to-do! Dreadful! . . . What did you say?
?
!
I say, Professor, why are you using the Captain's pipe for an ear-trumpet? . . . The Captain's pipe! . . . THE CAPTAIN'S PIPE!
?
Well, I never, it's the Captain's pipe! . . . I thought I wasn't hearing very well . . .
It's in here! Quick, use the foam.
You thundering nitwitted sea-gherkins!

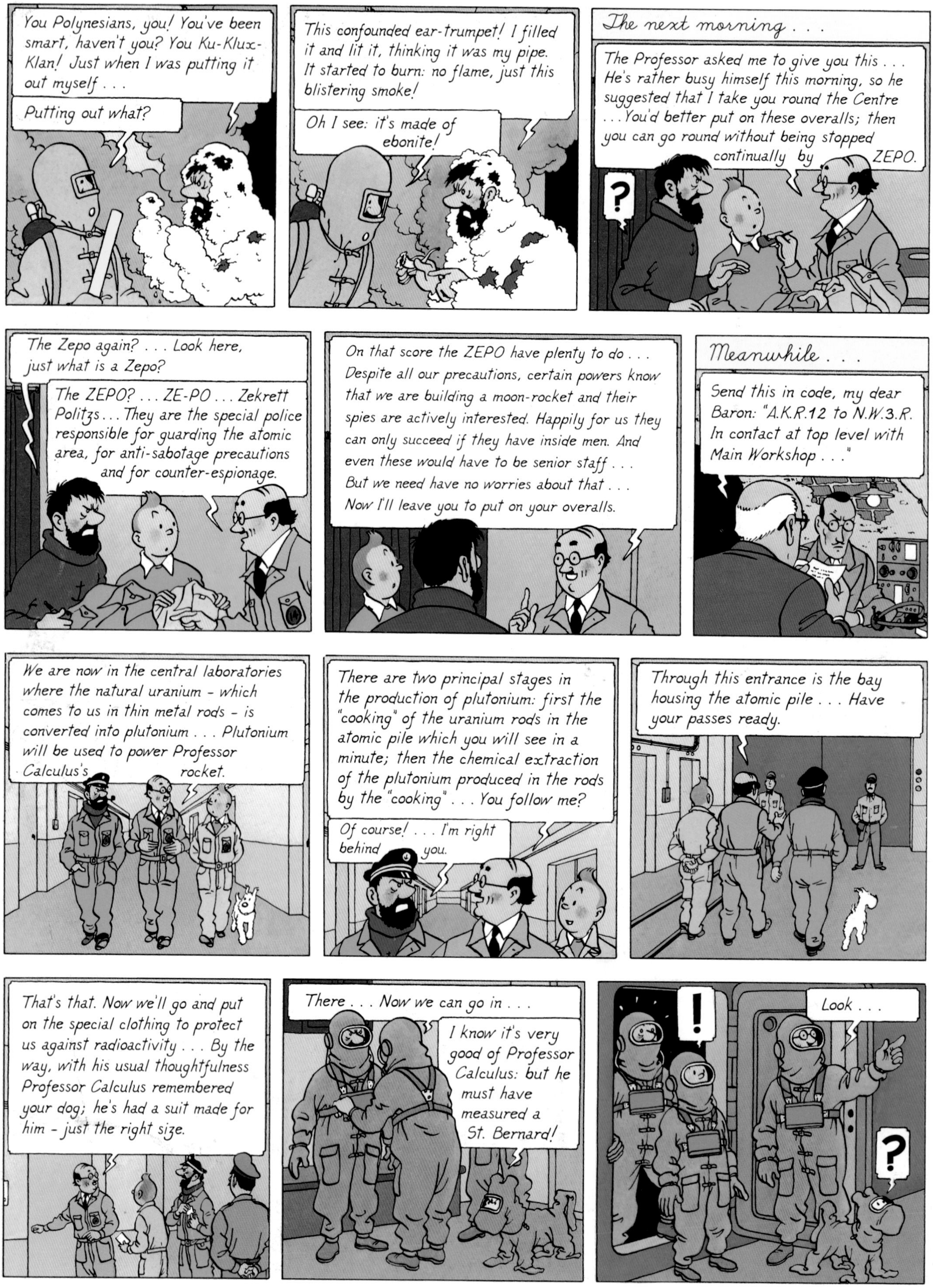
You Polynesians, you! You've been smart, haven't you? You Ku-Klux-Klan! Just when I was putting it out myself . . .
Putting out what?
This confounded ear-trumpet! I filled it and lit it, thinking it was my pipe. It started to burn: no flame, just this blistering smoke!
Oh I see: it's made of ebonite!
The next morning . . .
The Professor asked me to give you this . . . He's rather busy himself this morning, so he suggested that I take you round the Centre . . . You'd better put on these overalls; then you can go round without being stopped continually by ZEPO.
?
The Zepo again? . . . Look here, just what is a Zepo?
The ZEPO? . . . ZE-PO . . . Zekrett Politzs . . . They are the special police responsible for guarding the atomic area, for anti-sabotage precautions and for counter-espionage.
On that score the ZEPO have plenty to do . . . Despite all our precautions, certain powers know that we are building a moon-rocket and their spies are actively interested. Happily for us they can only succeed if they have inside men. And even these would have to be senior staff . . . But we need have no worries about that . . . Now I'll leave you to put on your overalls.
Meanwhile . . .
Send this in code, my dear Baron: "A.K.R.12 to N.W.3.R. In contact at top level with Main Workshop . . ."
We are now in the central laboratories where the natural uranium - which comes to us in thin metal rods - is converted into plutonium . . . Plutonium will be used to power Professor Calculus's rocket.
There are two principal stages in the production of plutonium: first the "cooking" of the uranium rods in the atomic pile which you will see in a minute; then the chemical extraction of the plutonium produced in the rods by the "cooking" . . . You follow me?
Of course! . . . I'm right behind you.
Through this entrance is the bay housing the atomic pile . . . Have your passes ready.
That's that. Now we'll go and put on the special clothing to protect us against radioactivity . . . By the way, with his usual thoughtfulness Professor Calculus remembered your dog; he's had a suit made for him - just the right size.
There . . . Now we can go in . . .
I know it's very good of Professor Calculus: but he must have measured a St. Bernard!
!
Look . . .
?

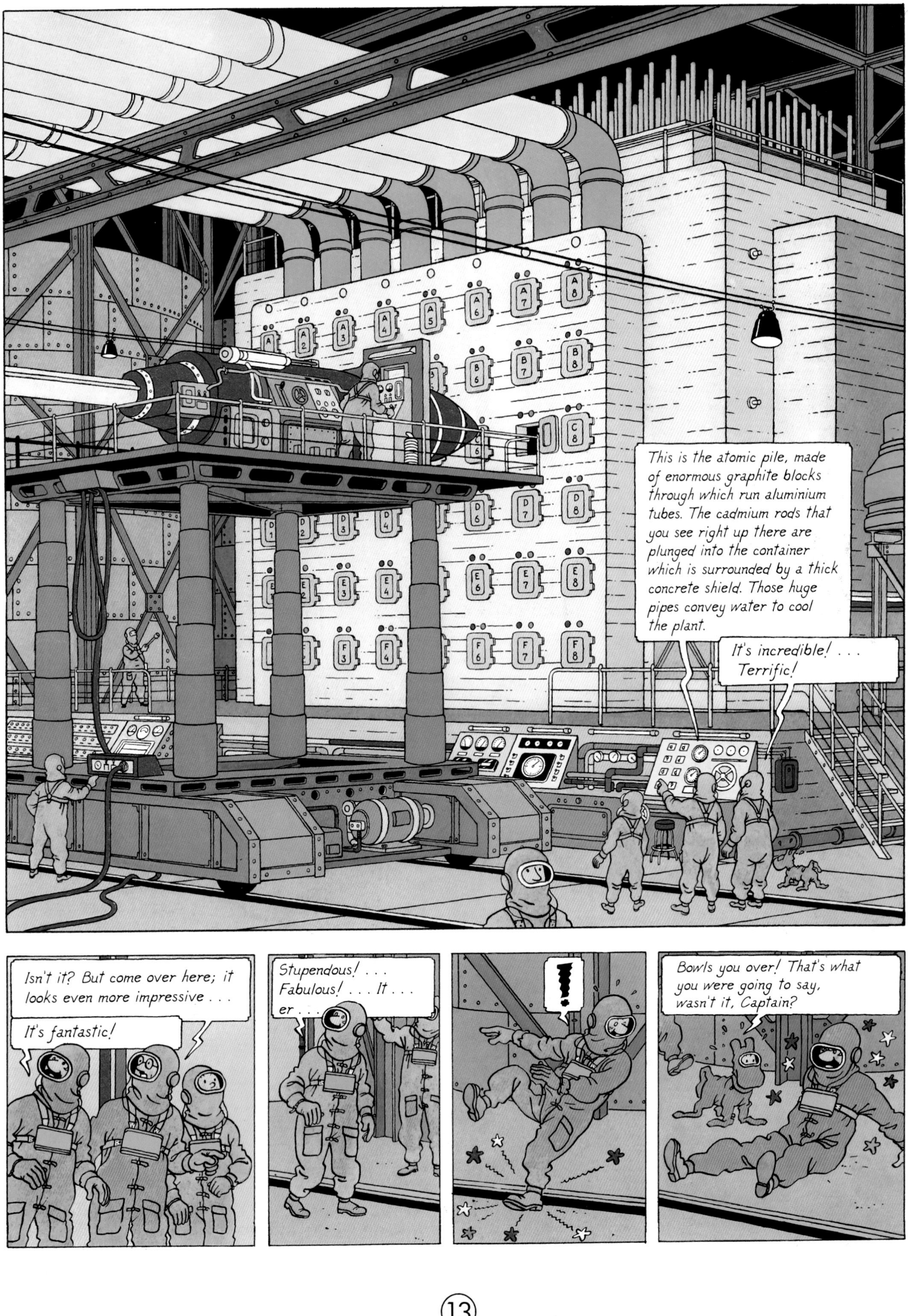
This is the atomic pile, made of enormous graphite blocks through which run aluminium tubes. The cadmium rods that you see right up there are plunged into the container which is surrounded by a thick concrete shield. Those huge pipes convey water to cool the plant.
It's incredible! . . . Terrific!
Isn't it? But come over here; it looks even more impressive . . .
It's fantastic!
Stupendous! . . . Fabulous! . . . It . . . er . . .
!
Bowls you over! That's what you were going to say, wasn't it, Captain?

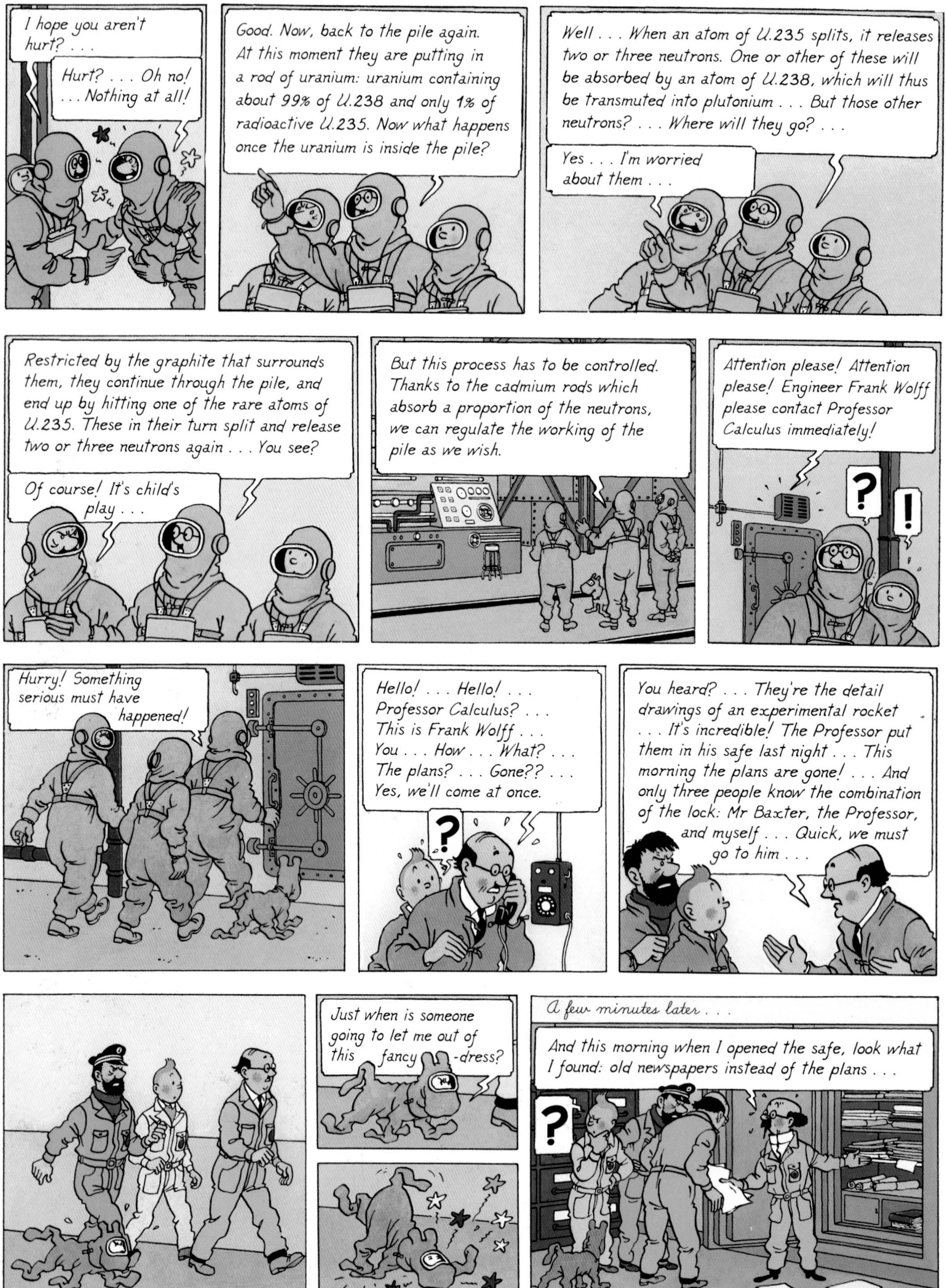
I hope you aren't hurt? . . .
Hurt? . . . Oh no! . . . Nothing at all!
Good. Now, back to the pile again. At this moment they are putting in a rod of uranium: uranium containing about 99% of U.238 and only 1% of radioactive U.235. Now what happens once the uranium is inside the pile?
Well . . . When an atom of U.235 splits, it releases two or three neutrons. One or other of these will be absorbed by an atom of U.238, which will thus be transmuted into plutonium . . . But those other neutrons? . . . Where will they go? . . .
Yes . . . I'm worried about them . . .
Restricted by the graphite that surrounds them, they continue through the pile, and end up by hitting one of the rare atoms of U.235. These in their turn split and release two or three neutrons again . . . You see?
Of course! It's child's play . . .
But this process has to be controlled. Thanks to the cadmium rods which absorb a proportion of the neutrons, we can regulate the working of the pile as we wish.
Attention please! Attention please! Engineer Frank Wolff please contact Professor Calculus immediately!
?
!
Hurry! Something serious must have happened!
Hello! . . . Hello! . . . Professor Calculus? . . . This is Frank Wolff . . . You . . . How . . . What? . . . The plans? . . . Gone?? . . . Yes, we'll come at once.
?
You heard? . . . They're the detail drawings of an experimental rocket . . . It's incredible! The Professor put them in his safe last night . . . This morning the plans are gone! . . . And only three people know the combination of the lock: Mr Baxter, the Professor, and myself . . . Quick, we must go to him . . .
Just when is someone going to let me out of this fancy-dress?
A few minutes later . . .
And this morning when I opened the safe, look what I found: old newspapers instead of the plans . . .
?

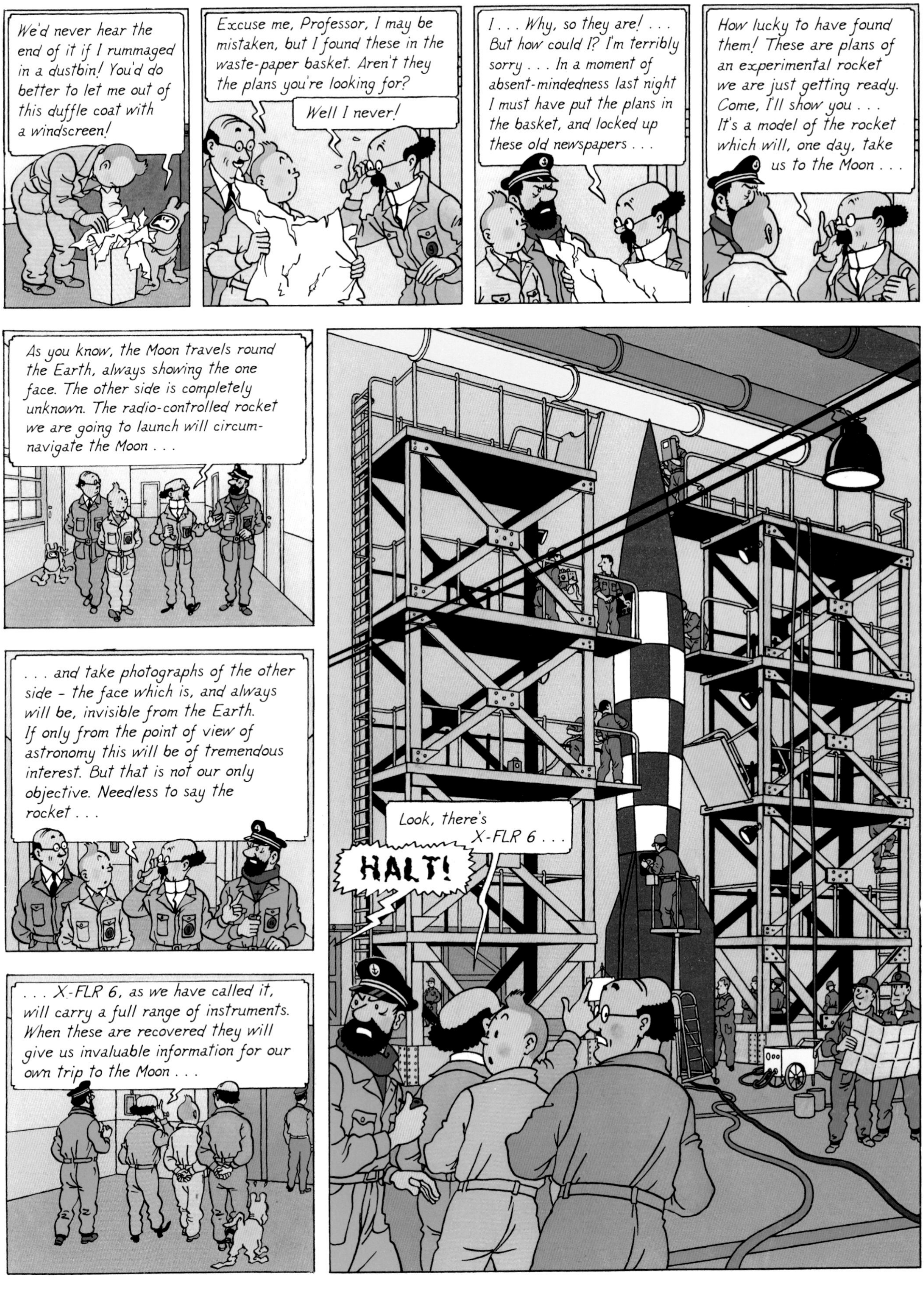

We'd never hear the end of it if I rummaged in a dustbin! You'd do better to let me out of this duffle coat with a windscreen!
Excuse me, Professor, I may be mistaken, but I found these in the waste-paper basket. Aren't they the plans you're looking for?
Well I never!
I . . . Why, so they are! . . . But how could I? I'm terribly sorry . . . In a moment of absent-mindedness last night I must have put the plans in the basket, and locked up these old newspapers . . .
How lucky to have found them! These are plans of an experimental rocket we are just getting ready. Come, I'll show you . . . It's a model of the rocket which will, one day, take us to the Moon . . .
As you know, the Moon travels round the Earth, always showing the one face. The other side is completely unknown. The radio-controlled rocket we are going to launch will circum-navigate the Moon . . .
. . . and take photographs of the other side - the face which is, and always will be, invisible from the Earth. If only from the point of view of astronomy this will be of tremendous interest. But that is not our only objective. Needless to say the rocket . . .
. . . X-FLR 6, as we have called it, will carry a full range of instruments. When these are recovered they will give us invaluable information for our own trip to the Moon . . .
Look, there's X-FLR 6 . . .
HALT!

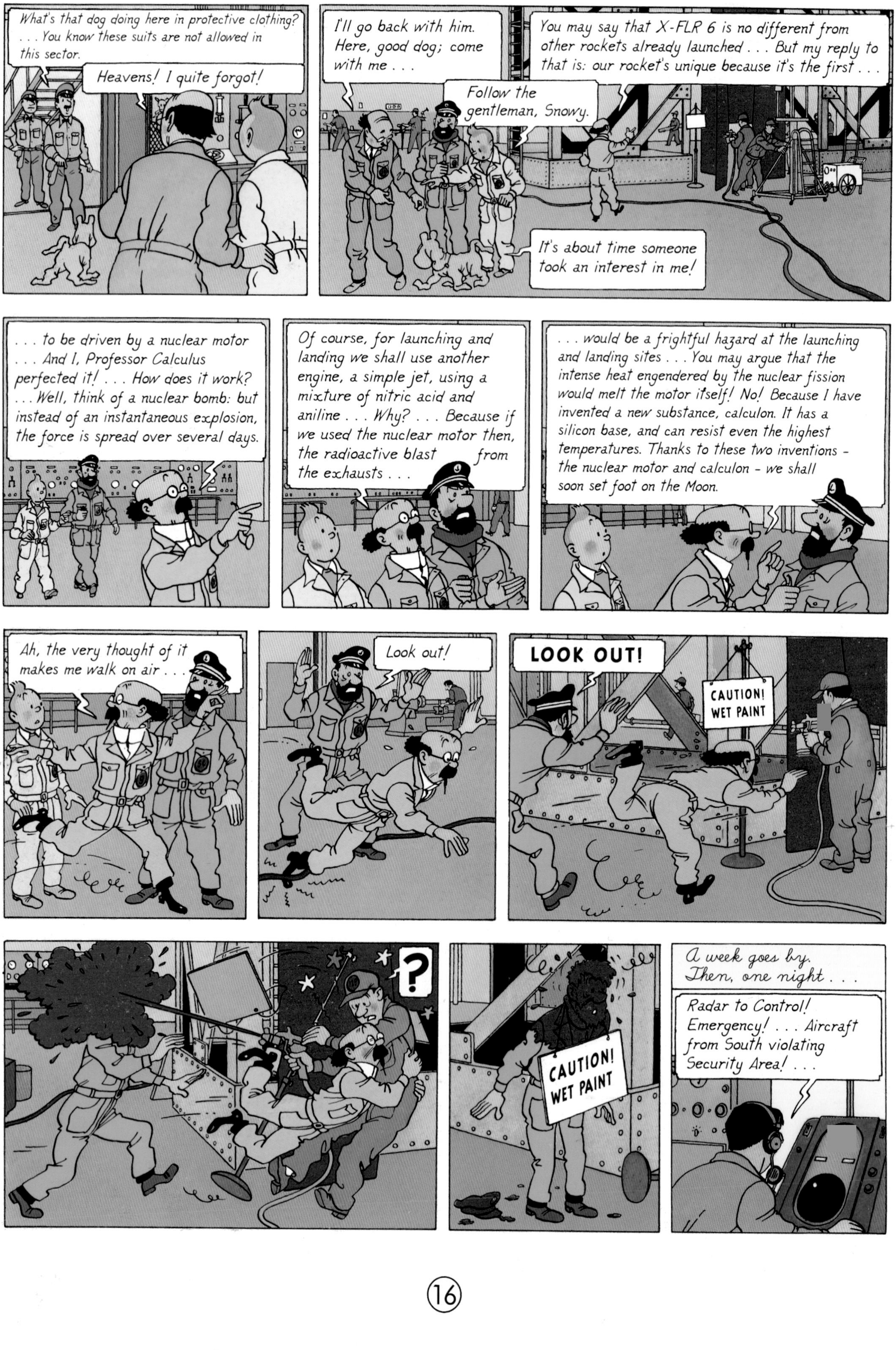
What's that dog doing here in protective clothing? . . . You know these suits are not allowed in this sector.
Heavens! I quite forgot!
I'll go back with him. Here, good dog; come with me . . .
Follow the gentleman, Snowy.
You may say that X-FLR 6 is no different from other rockets already launched . . . But my reply to that is: our rocket's unique because it's the first . . .
It's about time someone took an interest in me!
. . . to be driven by a nuclear motor . . . And I, Professor Calculus perfected it! . . . How does it work? . . . Well, think of a nuclear bomb: but instead of an instantaneous explosion, the force is spread over several days.
Of course, for launching and landing we shall use another engine, a simple jet, using a mixture of nitric acid and aniline . . . Why? . . . Because if we used the nuclear motor then, the radioactive blast from the exhausts . . .
. . . would be a frightful hazard at the launching and landing sites . . . You may argue that the intense heat engendered by the nuclear fission would melt the motor itself! No! Because I have invented a new substance, calculon. It has a silicon base, and can resist even the highest temperatures. Thanks to these two inventions - the nuclear motor and calculon - we shall soon set foot on the Moon.
Ah, the very thought of it makes me walk on air . . .
Look out!
LOOK OUT!
CAUTION! WET PAINT
?
CAUTION! WET PAINT
A week goes by. Then, one night . . .
Radar to Control! Emergency! . . . Aircraft from South violating Security Area! . . .

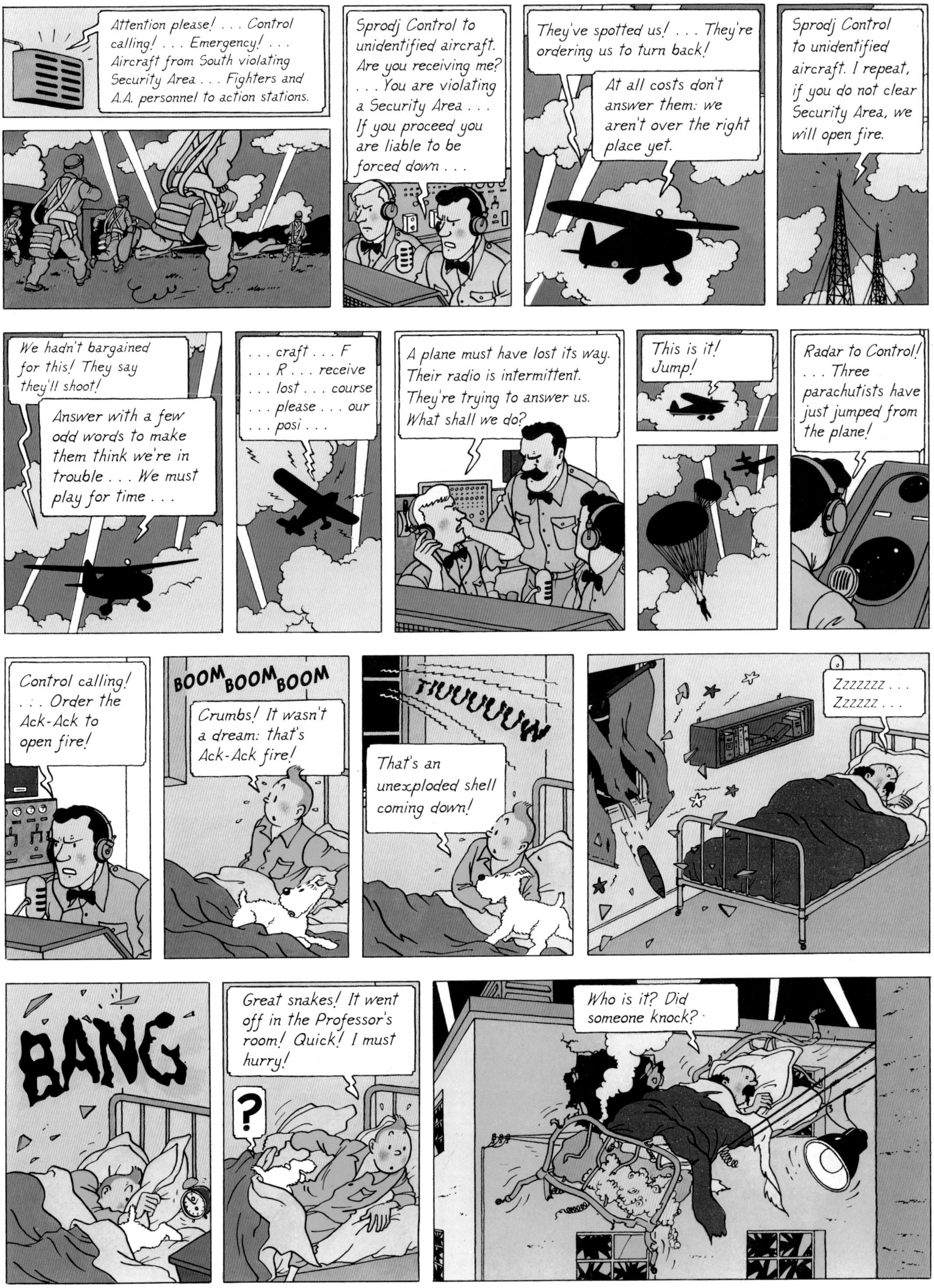

Attention please! . . . Control calling! . . . Emergency! . . . Aircraft from South violating Security Area . . . Fighters and A.A. personnel to action stations.
Sprodj Control to unidentified aircraft. Are you receiving me? . . . You are violating a Security Area . . . If you proceed you are liable to be forced down . . .
They've spotted us! . . . They're ordering us to turn back!
At all costs don't answer them: we aren't over the right place yet.
Sprodj Control to unidentified aircraft. I repeat, if you do not clear Security Area, we will open fire.
We hadn't bargained for this! They say they'll shoot!
Answer with a few odd words to make them think we're in trouble . . . We must play for time . . .
. . . craft . . . F . . . R . . . receive . . . lost . . . course . . . please . . . our . . . posi . . .
A plane must have lost its way. Their radio is intermittent. They're trying to answer us. What shall we do?
This is it! Jump!
Radar to Control! . . . Three parachutists have just jumped from the plane!
Control calling! . . . Order the Ack-Ack to open fire!
BOOM BOOM BOOM
Crumbs! It wasn't a dream: that's Ack-Ack fire!
TIUUUUUW
That's an unexploded shell coming down!
Zzzzzzz . . . Zzzzzz . . .
BANG
Great snakes! It went off in the Professor's room! Quick! I must hurry!
?
Who is it? Did someone knock?

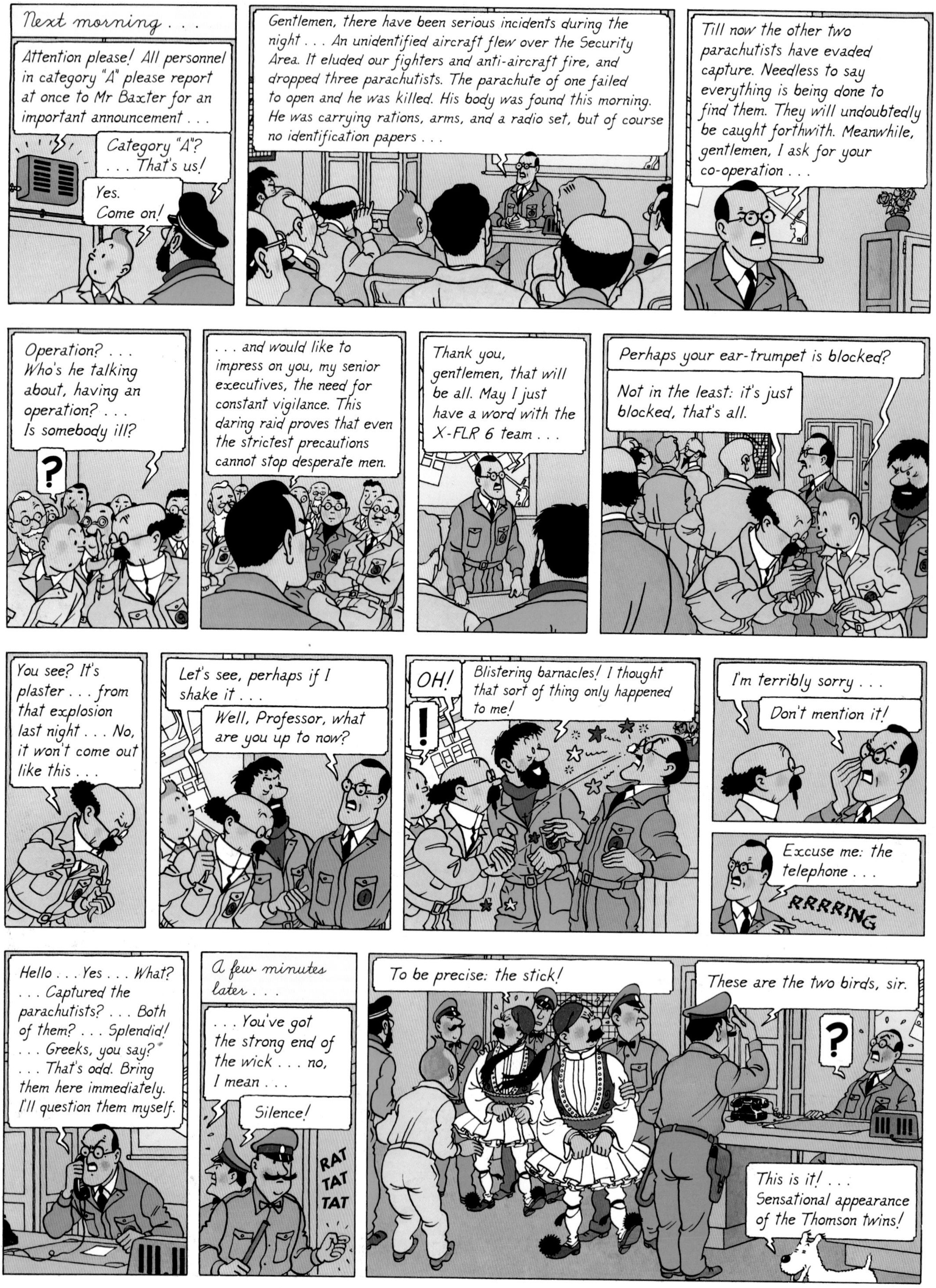

Next morning . . .
Attention please! All personnel in category "A" please report at once to Mr Baxter for an important announcement . . .
Category "A"? . . . That's us!
Yes. Come on!
Gentlemen, there have been serious incidents during the night . . . An unidentified aircraft flew over the Security Area. It eluded our fighters and anti-aircraft fire, and dropped three parachutists. The parachute of one failed to open and he was killed. His body was found this morning. He was carrying rations, arms, and a radio set, but of course no identification papers . . .
Till now the other two parachutists have evaded capture. Needless to say everything is being done to find them. They will undoubtedly be caught forthwith. Meanwhile, gentlemen, I ask for your co-operation . . .
Operation? . . . Who's he talking about, having an operation? . . . Is somebody ill?
?
. . . and would like to impress on you, my senior executives, the need for constant vigilance. This daring raid proves that even the strictest precautions cannot stop desperate men.
Thank you, gentlemen, that will be all. May I just have a word with the X-FLR 6 team . . .
Perhaps your ear-trumpet is blocked?
Not in the least: it's just blocked, that's all.
You see? It's plaster . . . from that explosion last night . . . No, it won't come out like this . . .
Let's see, perhaps if I shake it . . .
Well, Professor, what are you up to now?
OH!
!
Blistering barnacles! I thought that sort of thing only happened to me!
I'm terribly sorry . . .
Don't mention it!
Excuse me: the telephone . . .
RRRRING
Hello . . . Yes . . . What? . . . Captured the parachutists? . . . Both of them? . . . Splendid! . . . Greeks, you say? . . . That's odd. Bring them here immediately. I'll question them myself.
A few minutes later . . .
. . . You've got the strong end of the wick . . . no, I mean . . .
Silence!
RAT TAT TAT
To be precise: the stick!
These are the two birds, sir.
?
This is it! . . . Sensational appearance of the Thomson twins!

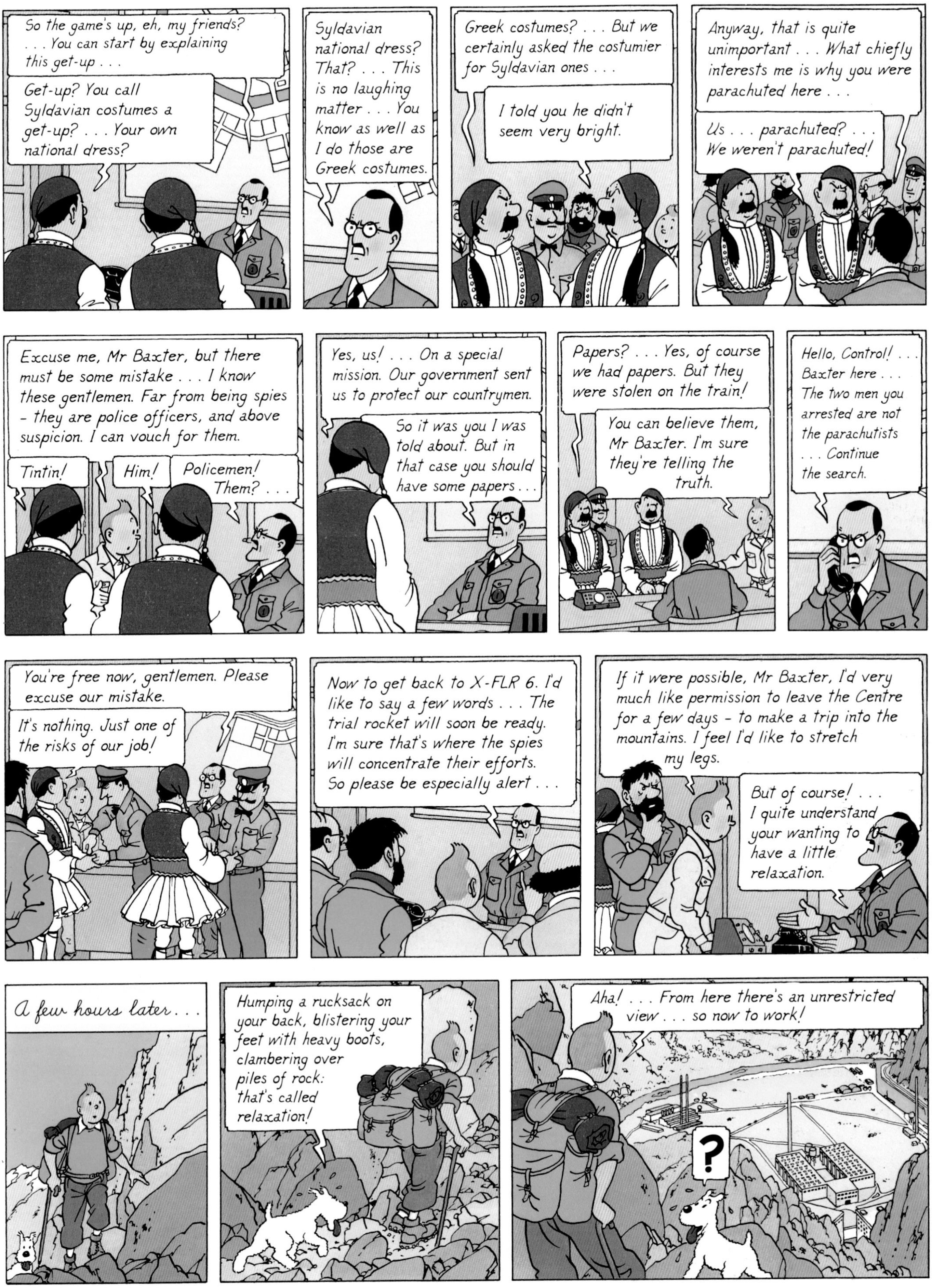
So the game's up, eh, my friends? . . . You can start by explaining this get-up . . .
Get-up? You call Syldavian costumes a get-up? . . . Your own national dress?
Syldavian national dress? That? . . . This is no laughing matter . . . You know as well as I do those are Greek costumes.
Greek costumes? . . . But we certainly asked the costumier for Syldavian ones . . .
I told you he didn't seem very bright.
Anyway, that is quite unimportant . . . What chiefly interests me is why you were parachuted here . . .
Us . . . parachuted? . . . We weren't parachuted!
Excuse me, Mr Baxter, but there must be some mistake . . . I know these gentlemen. Far from being spies - they are police officers, and above suspicion. I can vouch for them.
Tintin!
Him!
Policemen! Them? . . .
Yes, us! . . . On a special mission. Our government sent us to protect our countrymen.
So it was you I was told about. But in that case you should have some papers . . .
Papers? . . . Yes, of course we had papers. But they were stolen on the train!
You can believe them, Mr Baxter. I'm sure they're telling the truth.
Hello, Control! . . . Baxter here . . . The two men you arrested are not the parachutists . . . Continue the search.
You're free now, gentlemen. Please excuse our mistake.
It's nothing. Just one of the risks of our job!
Now to get back to X-FLR 6. I'd like to say a few words . . . The trial rocket will soon be ready. I'm sure that's where the spies will concentrate their efforts. So please be especially alert . . .
If it were possible, Mr Baxter, I'd very much like permission to leave the Centre for a few days - to make a trip into the mountains. I feel I'd like to stretch my legs.
But of course! . . . I quite understand your wanting to have a little relaxation.
A few hours later . . .
Humping a rucksack on your back, blistering your feet with heavy boots, clambering over piles of rock: that's called relaxation!
Aha! . . . From here there's an unrestricted view . . . so now to work!
?

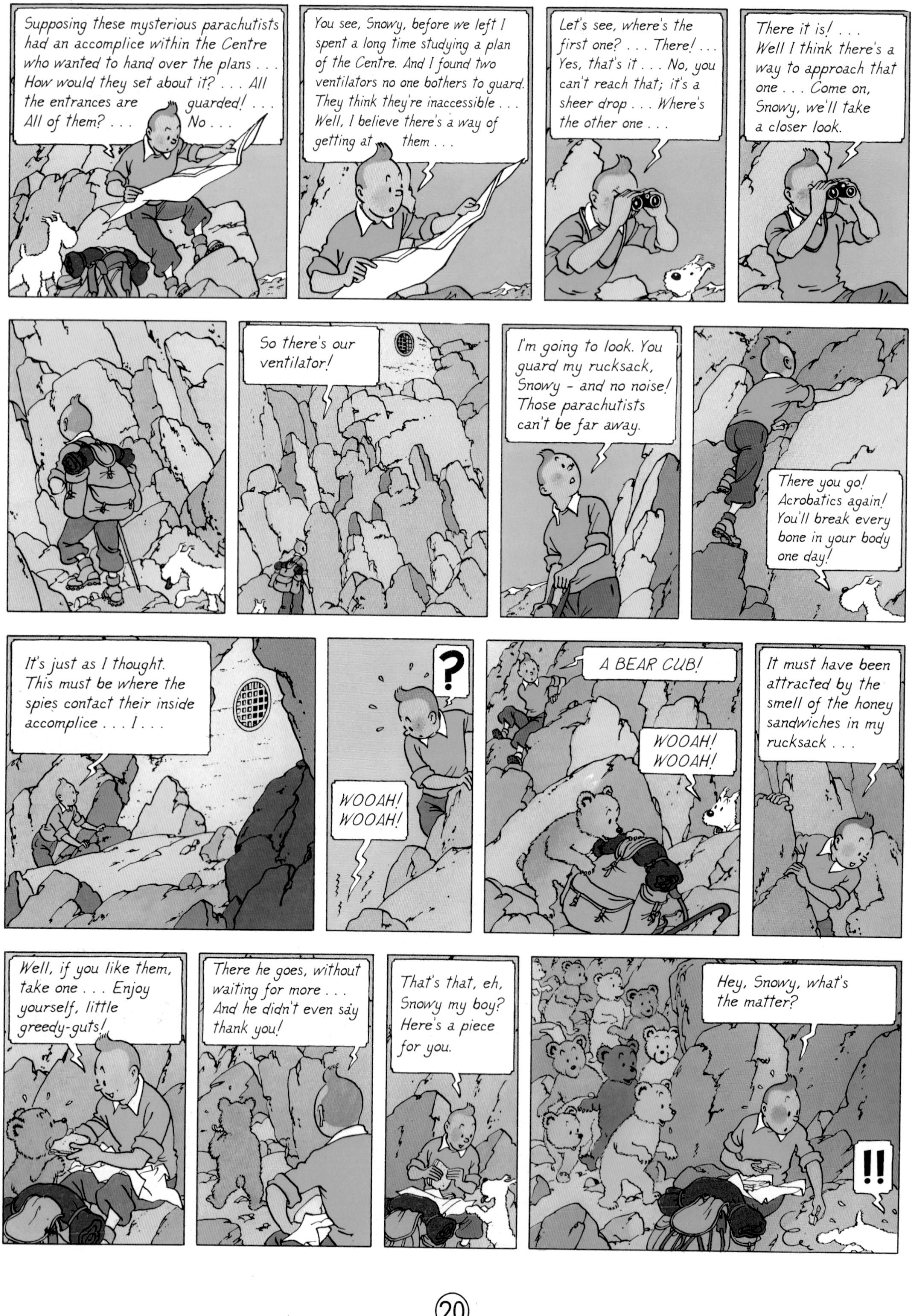
Supposing these mysterious parachutists had an accomplice within the Centre who wanted to hand over the plans . . . How would they set about it? . . . All the entrances are guarded! . . . All of them? . . . No . . .
You see, Snowy, before we left I spent a long time studying a plan of the Centre. And I found two ventilators no one bothers to guard. They think they're inaccessible . . . Well, I believe there's a way of getting at them . . .
Let's see, where's the first one? . . . There! . . . Yes, that's it . . . No, you can't reach that; it's a sheer drop . . . Where's the other one . . .
There it is! . . . Well I think there's a way to approach that one . . . Come on, Snowy, we'll take a closer look.
So there's our ventilator!
I'm going to look. You guard my rucksack, Snowy - and no noise! Those parachutists can't be far away.
There you go! Acrobatics again! You'll break every bone in your body one day!
It's just as I thought. This must be where the spies contact their inside accomplice . . . I . . .
?
WOOAH! WOOAH!
A BEAR CUB!
WOOAH! WOOAH!
It must have been attracted by the smell of the honey sandwiches in my rucksack . . .
Well, if you like them, take one . . . Enjoy yourself, little greedy-guts!
There he goes, without waiting for more . . . And he didn't even say thank you!
That's that, eh, Snowy my boy? Here's a piece for you.
Hey, Snowy, what's the matter?
!!

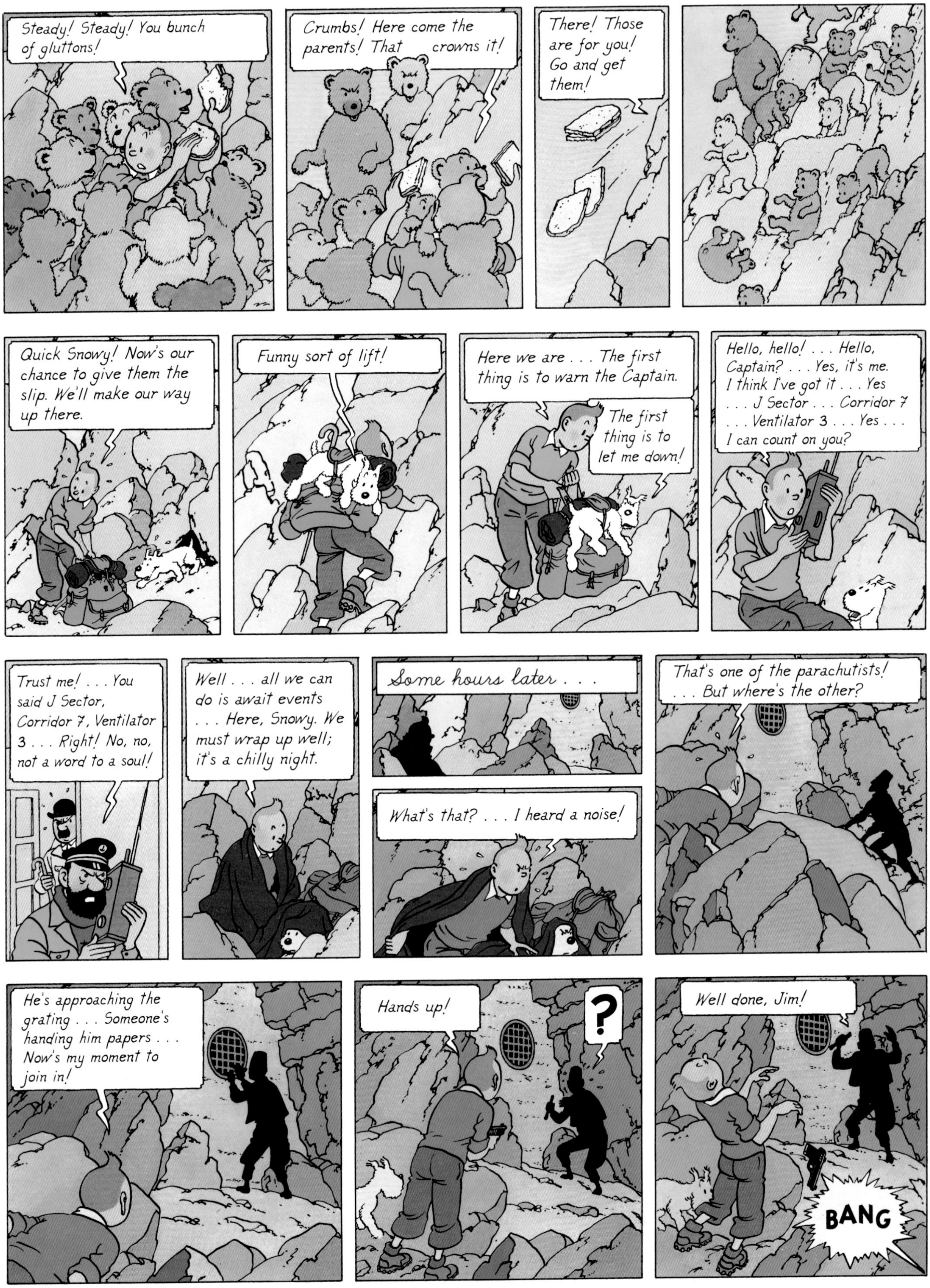

Steady! Steady! You bunch of gluttons!
Crumbs! Here come the parents! That crowns it!
There! Those are for you! Go and get them!
Quick Snowy! Now's our chance to give them the slip. We'll make our way up there.
Funny sort of lift!
Here we are . . . The first thing is to warn the Captain.
The first thing is to let me down!
Hello, hello! . . . Hello, Captain? . . . Yes, it's me. I think I've got it . . . Yes . . . J Sector . . . Corridor 7 . . . Ventilator 3 . . . Yes . . . I can count on you?
Trust me! . . . You said J Sector, Corridor 7, Ventilator 3 . . . Right! No, no, not a word to a soul!
Well . . . all we can do is await events . . . Here, Snowy. We must wrap up well; it's a chilly night.
Some hours later . . .
What's that? . . . I heard a noise!
That's one of the parachutists! . . . But where's the other?
He's approaching the grating . . . Someone's handing him papers . . . Now's my moment to join in!
Hands up!
?
Well done, Jim!
BANG

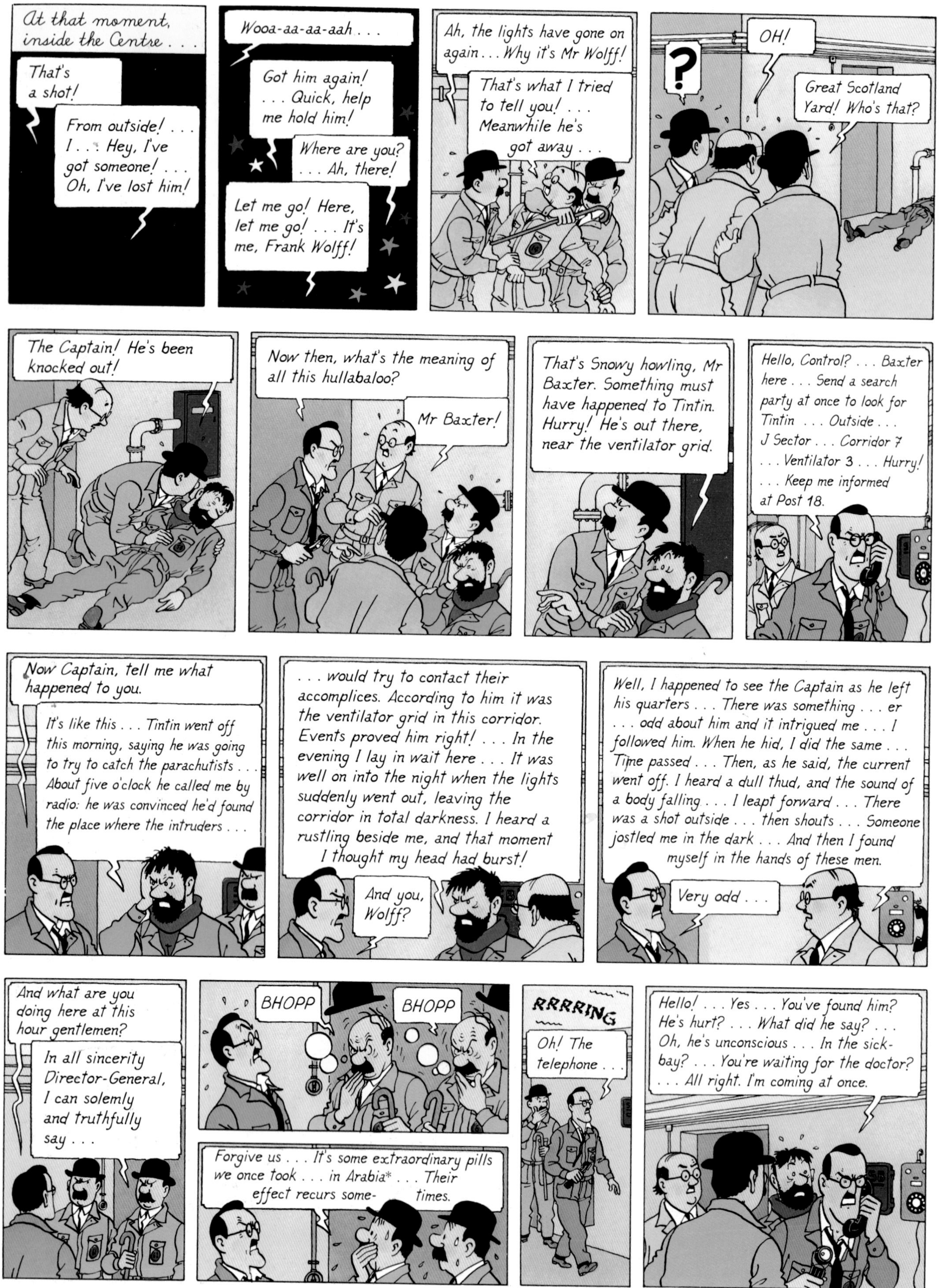
At that moment, inside the Centre . . .
That's a shot!
From outside! . . . I . . . Hey, I've got someone! . . . Oh, I've lost him!
Wooa-aa-aa-aah . . .
Got him again! . . . Quick, help me hold him!
Where are you? . . . Ah, there!
Let me go! Here, let me go! . . . It's me, Frank Wolff!
Ah, the lights have gone on again . . . Why it's Mr Wolff!
That's what I tried to tell you! . . . Meanwhile he's got away . . .
?
OH!
Great Scotland Yard! Who's that?
The Captain! He's been knocked out!
Now then, what's the meaning of all this hullabaloo?
Mr Baxter!
That's Snowy howling, Mr Baxter. Something must have happened to Tintin. Hurry! He's out there, near the ventilator grid.
Hello, Control? . . . Baxter here . . . Send a search party at once to look for Tintin . . . Outside . . . J Sector . . . Corridor 7 . . . Ventilator 3 . . . Hurry! . . . Keep me informed at Post 18.
Now Captain, tell me what happened to you.
It's like this . . . Tintin went off this morning, saying he was going to try to catch the parachutists . . . About five o'clock he called me by radio: he was convinced he'd found the place where the intruders . . .
. . . would try to contact their accomplices. According to him it was the ventilator grid in this corridor. Events proved him right! . . . In the evening I lay in wait here . . . It was well on into the night when the lights suddenly went out, leaving the corridor in total darkness. I heard a rustling beside me, and that moment I thought my head had burst!
And you, Wolff?
Well, I happened to see the Captain as he left his quarters . . . There was something . . . er . . . odd about him and it intrigued me . . . I followed him. When he hid, I did the same . . . Time passed . . . Then, as he said, the current went off. I heard a dull thud, and the sound of a body falling . . . I leapt forward . . . There was a shot outside . . . then shouts . . . Someone jostled me in the dark . . . And then I found myself in the hands of these men.
Very odd . . .
And what are you doing here at this hour gentlemen?
In all sincerity Director-General, I can solemly and truthfully say . . .
BHOPP
BHOPP
Forgive us . . . It's some extraordinary pills we once took . . . in Arabia* . . . Their effect recurs some- times.
RRRRING
Oh! The telephone . . .
Hello! . . . Yes . . . You've found him? He's hurt? . . . What did he say? . . . Oh, he's unconscious . . . In the sick-bay? . . . You're waiting for the doctor? . . . All right. I'm coming at once.

*See Land of Black Gold

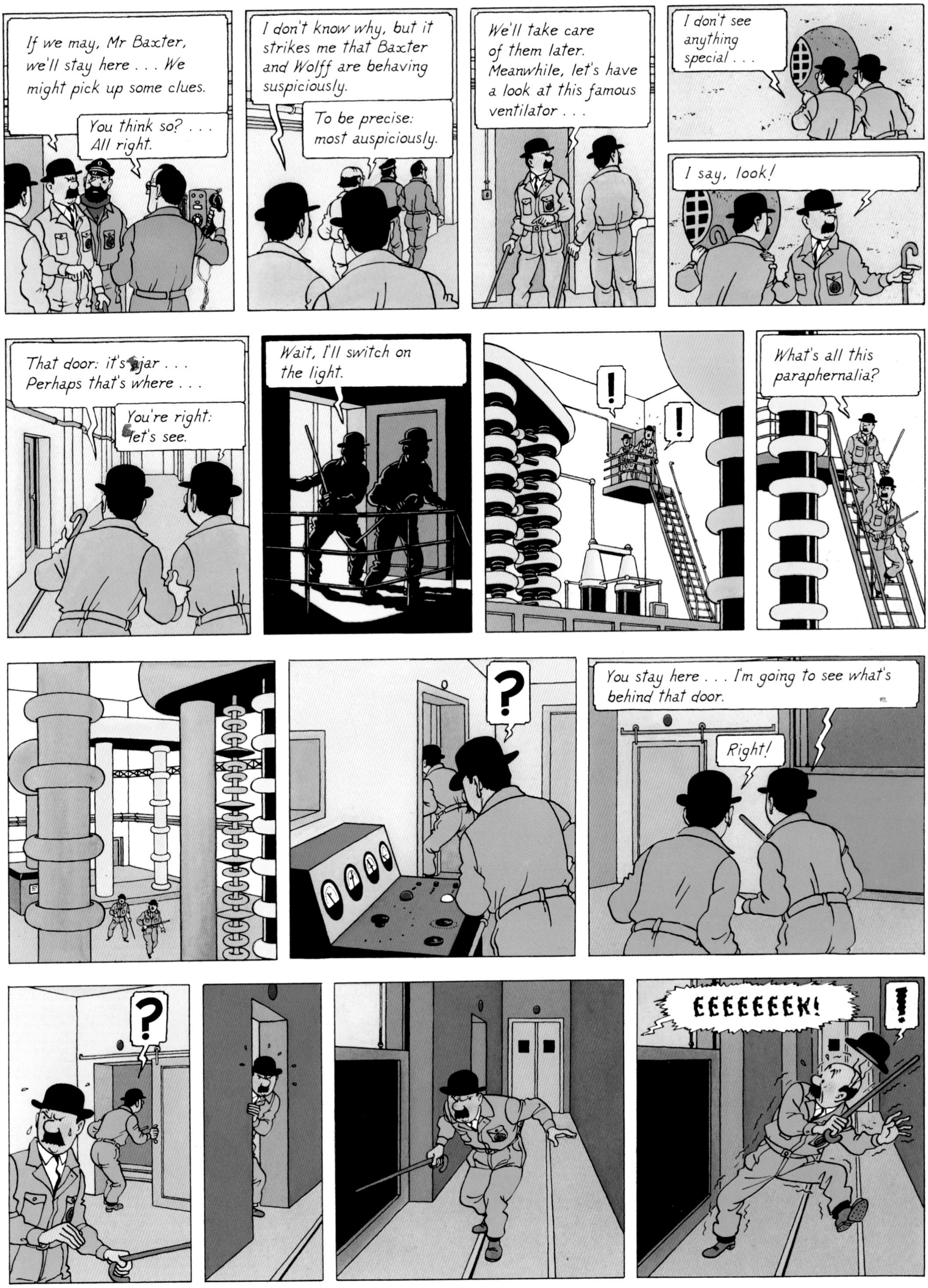
If we may, Mr Baxter, we'll stay here . . . We might pick up some clues.
You think so? . . . All right.
I don't know why, but it strikes me that Baxter and Wolff are behaving suspiciously.
To be precise: most auspiciously.
We'll take care of them later. Meanwhile, let's have a look at this famous ventilator . . .
I don't see anything special . . .
I say, look!
That door: it's ajar . . . Perhaps that's where . . .
You're right: let's see.
Wait, I'll switch on the light.
!
!
What's all this paraphernalia?
?
You stay here . . . I'm going to see what's behind that door.
Right!
?
EEEEEEEK!
!

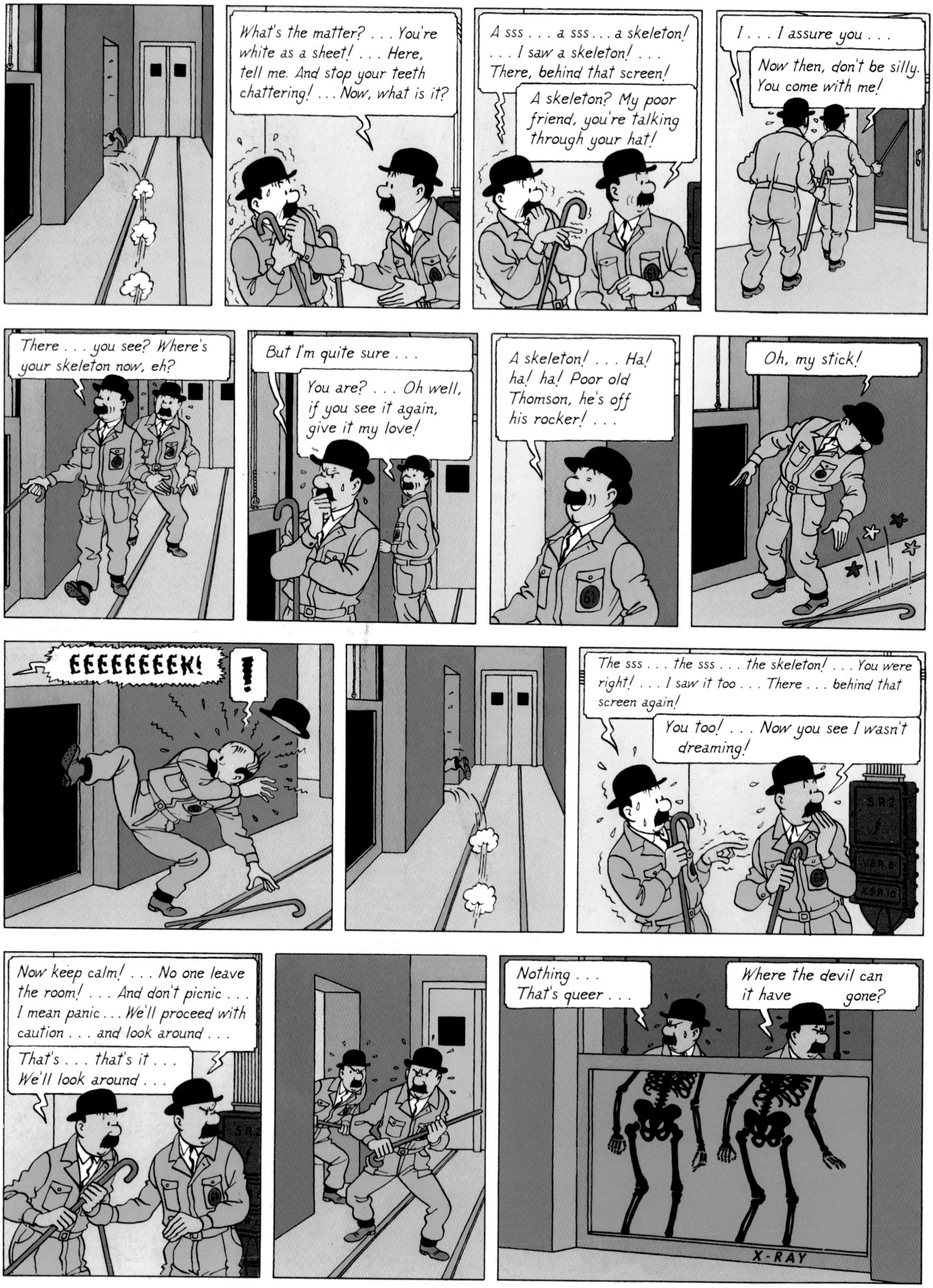
What's the matter? . . . You're white as a sheet! . . . Here, tell me. And stop your teeth chattering! . . . Now, what is it?
A sss . . . a sss . . . a skeleton! . . . I saw a skeleton! . . . There, behind that screen!
A skeleton? My poor friend, you're talking through your hat!
I . . . I assure you . . .
Now then, don't be silly. You come with me!
There . . . you see? Where's your skeleton now, eh?
But I'm quite sure . . .
You are? . . . Oh well, if you see it again, give it my love!
A skeleton! . . . Ha! ha! ha! Poor old Thomson, he's off his rocker! . . .
Oh, my stick!
EEEEEEEEEK!
!!!
The sss . . . the sss . . . the skeleton! . . . You were right! . . . I saw it too . . . There . . . behind that screen again!
You too! . . . Now you see I wasn't dreaming!
S.R.2
V.S.R.8
X.S.R.10
Now keep calm! . . . No one leave the room! . . . And don't picnic . . . I mean panic . . . We'll proceed with caution . . . and look around . . .
That's . . . that's it . . . We'll look around . . .
Nothing . . . That's queer . . .
Where the devil can it have gone?
X-RAY

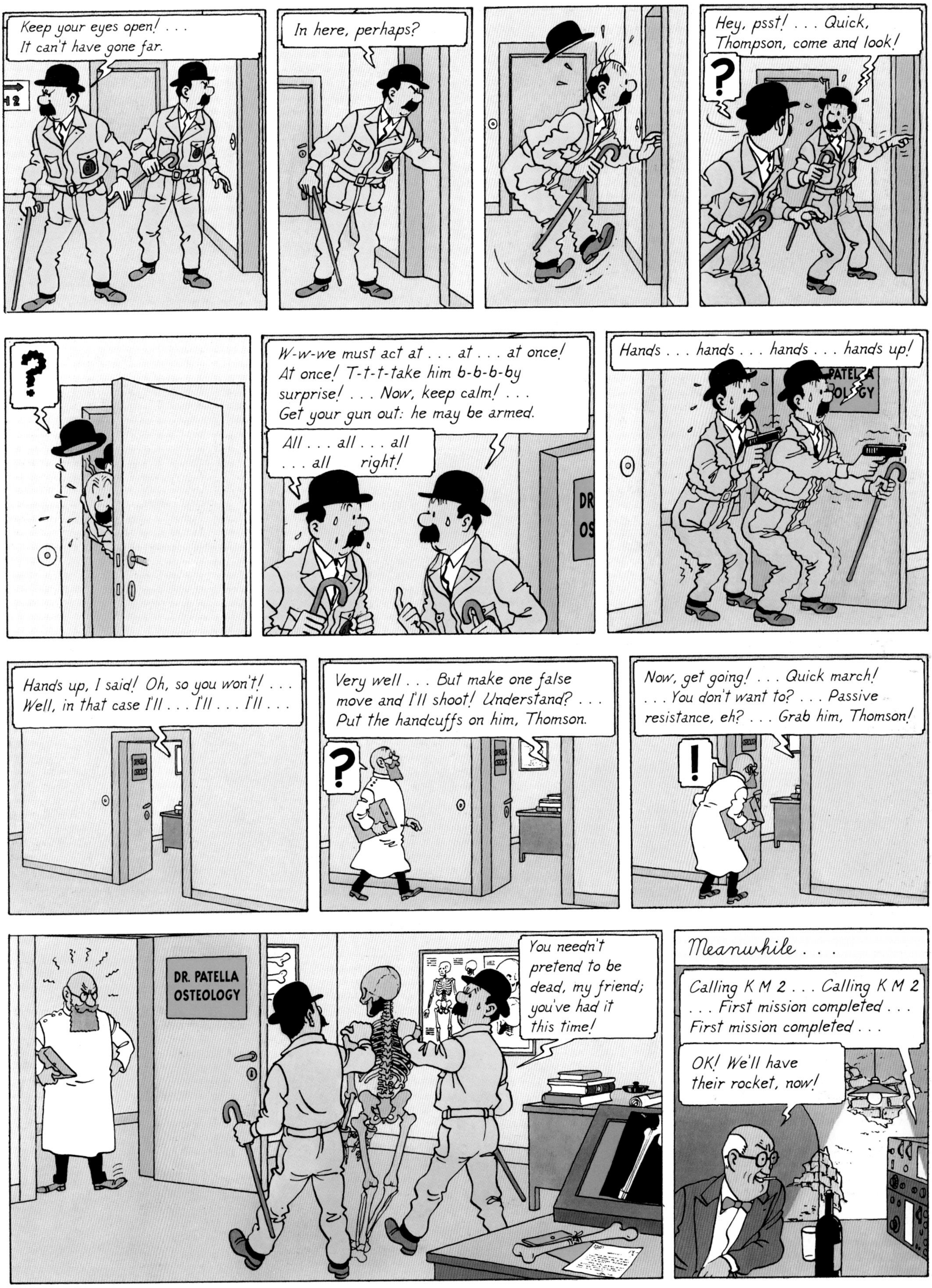

Keep your eyes open! . . . It can't have gone far.
In here, perhaps?
Hey, psst! . . . Quick, Thompson, come and look!
?
?
W-w-we must act at . . . at . . . at once! At once! T-t-t-take him b-b-b-by surprise! . . . Now, keep calm! . . . Get your gun out: he may be armed.
All . . . all . . . all . . . all right!
Hands . . . hands . . . hands . . . hands up!
Hands up, I said! Oh, so you won't! . . . Well, in that case I'll . . . I'll . . . I'll . . .
Very well . . . But make one false move and I'll shoot! Understand? . . . Put the handcuffs on him, Thomson.
?
Now, get going! . . . Quick march! . . . You don't want to? . . . Passive resistance, eh? . . . Grab him, Thomson!
!
DR. PATELLA OSTEOLOGY
You needn't pretend to be dead, my friend; you've had it this time!
Meanwhile . . .
Calling K M 2 . . . Calling K M 2 . . . First mission completed . . . First mission completed . . .
OK! We'll have their rocket, now!

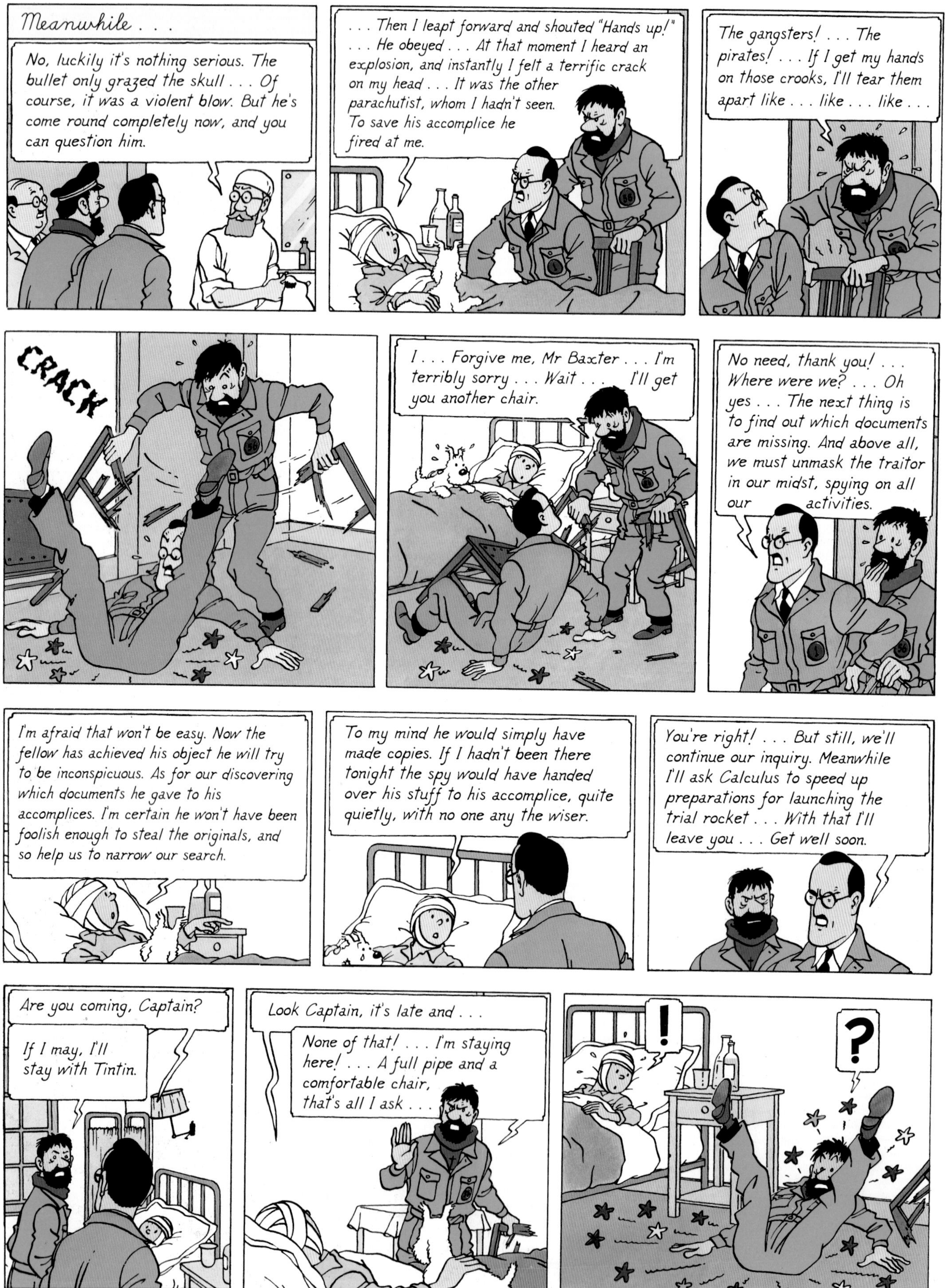
Meanwhile . . .
No, luckily it's nothing serious. The bullet only grazed the skull . . . Of course, it was a violent blow. But he's come round completely now, and you can question him.
. . . Then I leapt forward and shouted "Hands up!" . . . He obeyed . . . At that moment I heard an explosion, and instantly I felt a terrific crack on my head . . . It was the other parachutist, whom I hadn't seen. To save his accomplice he fired at me.
The gangsters! . . . The pirates! . . . If I get my hands on those crooks, I'll tear them apart like . . . like . . . like . . .
CRACK
I . . . Forgive me, Mr Baxter . . . I'm terribly sorry . . . Wait . . . I'll get you another chair.
No need, thank you! . . . Where were we? . . . Oh yes . . . The next thing is to find out which documents are missing. And above all, we must unmask the traitor in our midst, spying on all our activities.
I'm afraid that won't be easy. Now the fellow has achieved his object he will try to be inconspicuous. As for our discovering which documents he gave to his accomplices. I'm certain he won't have been foolish enough to steal the originals, and so help us to narrow our search.
To my mind he would simply have made copies. If I hadn't been there tonight the spy would have handed over his stuff to his accomplice, quite quietly, with no one any the wiser.
You're right! . . . But still, we'll continue our inquiry. Meanwhile I'll ask Calculus to speed up preparations for launching the trial rocket . . . With that I'll leave you . . . Get well soon.
Are you coming, Captain?
If I may, I'll stay with Tintin.
Look Captain, it's late and . . .
None of that! . . . I'm staying here! . . . A full pipe and a comfortable chair, that's all I ask . . .
!
?

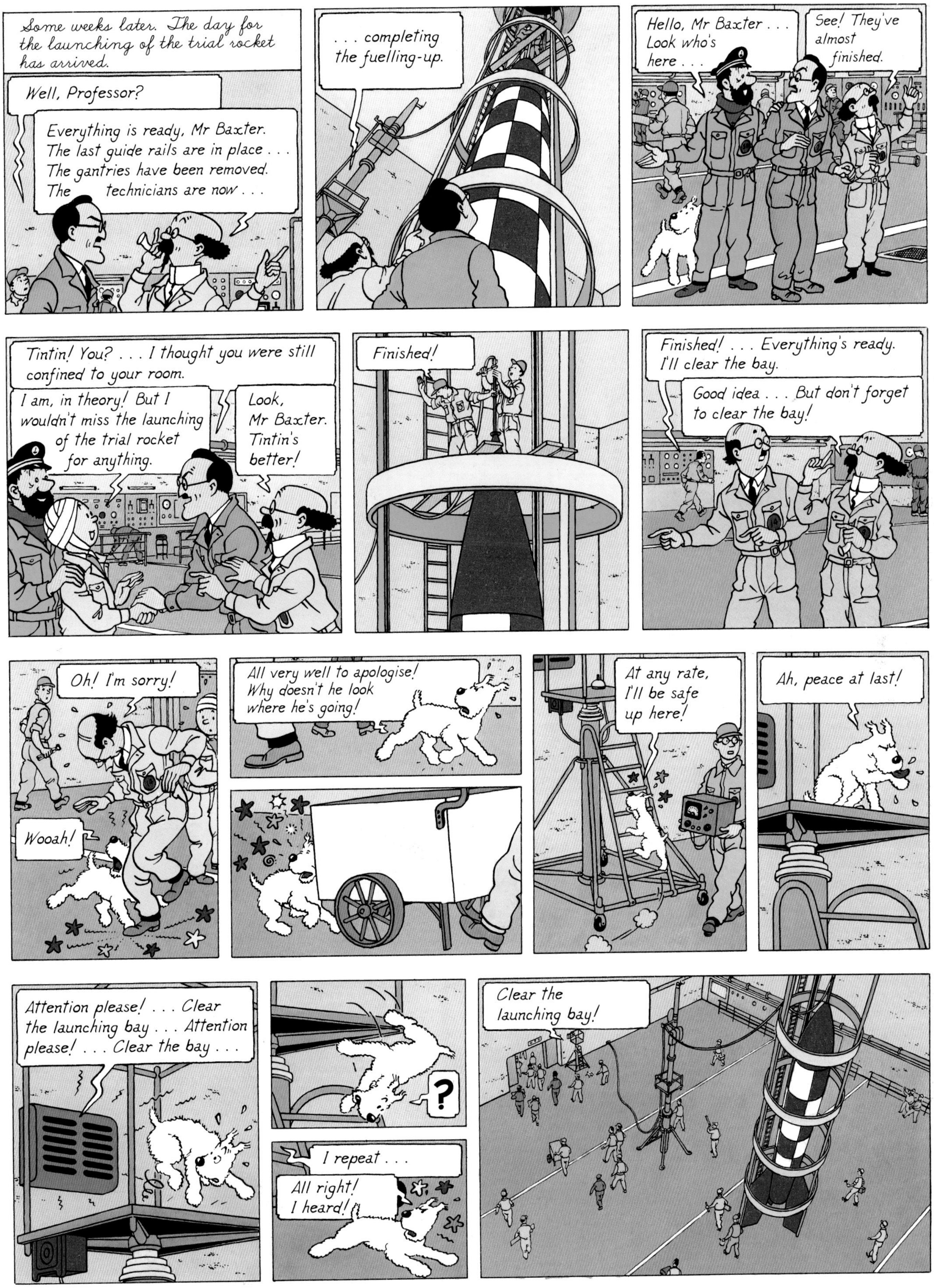
Some weeks later. The day for the launching of the trial rocket has arrived.
Well, Professor?
Everything is ready, Mr Baxter. The last guide rails are in place . . . The gantries have been removed. The technicians are now . . .
. . . completing the fuelling-up.
Hello, Mr Baxter . . . Look who's here . . .
See! They've almost finished.
Tintin! You? . . . I thought you were still confined to your room.
I am, in theory! But I wouldn't miss the launching of the trial rocket for anything.
Look, Mr Baxter. Tintin's better!
Finished!
Finished! . . . Everything's ready. I'll clear the bay.
Good idea . . . But don't forget to clear the bay!
Oh! I'm sorry!
Wooah!
All very well to apologise! Why doesn't he look where he's going!
At any rate, I'll be safe up here!
Ah, peace at last!
Attention please! . . . Clear the launching bay . . . Attention please! . . . Clear the bay . . .
?
I repeat . . .
All right! I heard!
Clear the launching bay!

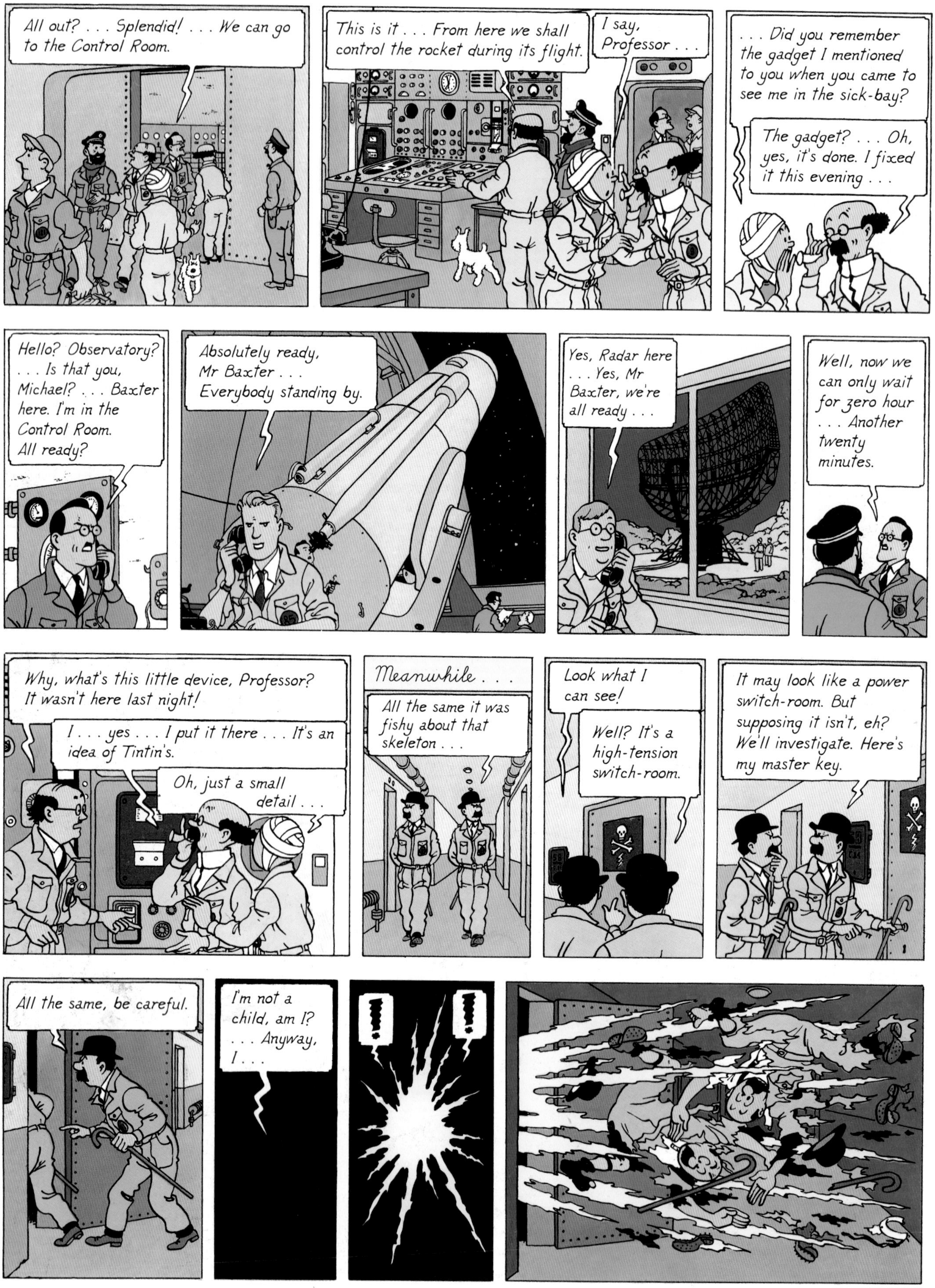

All out? . . . Splendid! . . . We can go to the Control Room.
This is it . . . From here we shall control the rocket during its flight.
I say, Professor . . .
. . . Did you remember the gadget I mentioned to you when you came to see me in the sick-bay?
The gadget? . . . Oh, yes, it's done. I fixed it this evening . . .
Hello? Observatory? . . . Is that you, Michael? . . . Baxter here. I'm in the Control Room. All ready?
Absolutely ready, Mr Baxter . . . Everybody standing by.
Yes, Radar here . . . Yes, Mr Baxter, we're all ready . . .
Well, now we can only wait for zero hour . . . Another twenty minutes.
Why, what's this little device, Professor? It wasn't here last night!
I . . . yes . . . I put it there . . . It's an idea of Tintin's.
Oh, just a small detail . . .
Meanwhile . . .
All the same it was fishy about that skeleton . . .
Look what I can see!
Well? It's a high-tension switch-room.
It may look like a power switch-room. But supposing it isn't, eh? We'll investigate. Here's my master key.
All the same, be careful.
I'm not a child, am I? . . . Anyway, I . . .

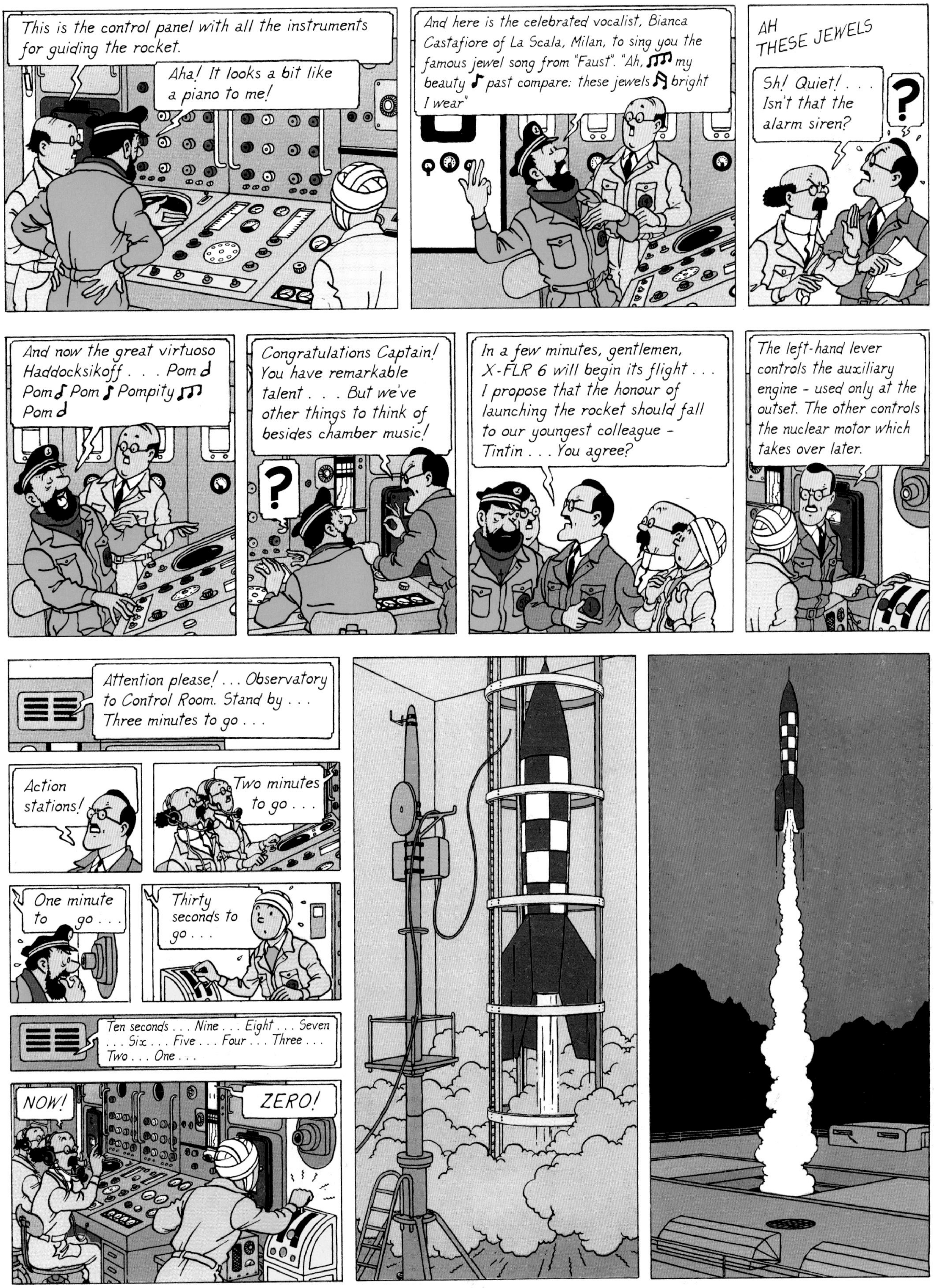
This is the control panel with all the instruments for guiding the rocket.
Aha! It looks a bit like a piano to me!
And here is the celebrated vocalist, Bianca Castafiore of La Scala, Milan, to sing you the famous jewel song from "Faust". "Ah, my beauty past compare: these jewels bright I wear"
AH THESE JEWELS
Sh! Quiet! . . . Isn't that the alarm siren?
?
And now the great virtuoso Haddocksikoff . . . Pom Pom Pom Pompity Pom
Congratulations Captain! You have remarkable talent . . . But we've other things to think of besides chamber music!
?
In a few minutes, gentlemen, X-FLR 6 will begin its flight . . . I propose that the honour of launching the rocket should fall to our youngest colleague - Tintin . . . You agree?
The left-hand lever controls the auxiliary engine - used only at the outset. The other controls the nuclear motor which takes over later.
Attention please! . . . Observatory to Control Room. Stand by . . . Three minutes to go . . .
Action stations!
Two minutes to go . . .
One minute to go . . .
Thirty seconds to go . . .
Ten seconds . . . Nine . . . Eight . . . Seven . . . Six . . . Five . . . Four . . . Three . . . Two . . . One . . .
NOW!
ZERO!

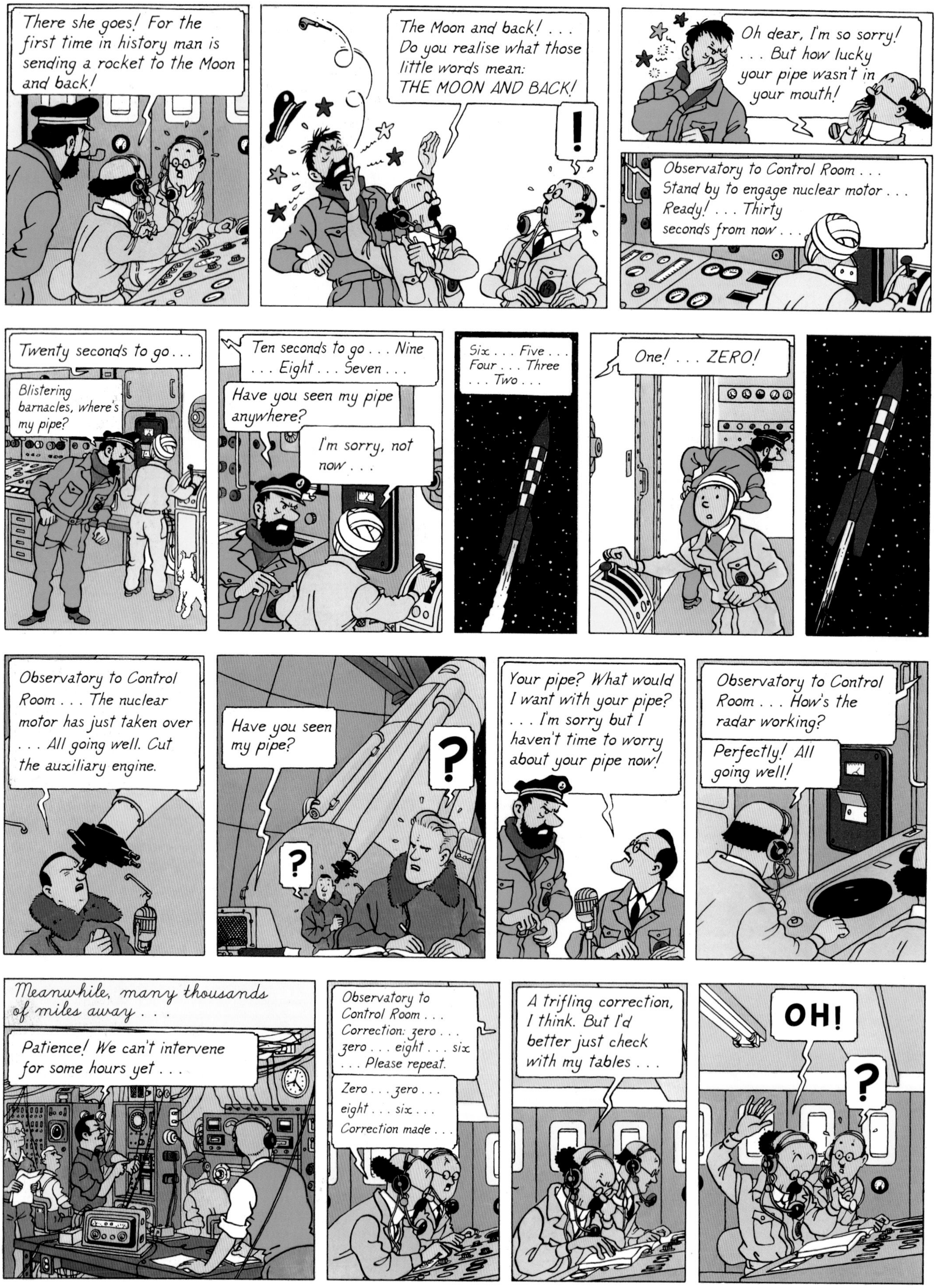
There she goes! For the first time in history man is sending a rocket to the Moon and back!
The Moon and back! . . . Do you realise what those little words mean: THE MOON AND BACK!
!
Oh dear, I'm so sorry! . . . But how lucky your pipe wasn't in your mouth!
Observatory to Control Room . . . Stand by to engage nuclear motor . . . Ready! . . . Thirty seconds from now . . .
Twenty seconds to go . . .
Blistering barnacles, where's my pipe?
Ten seconds to go . . . Nine . . . Eight . . . Seven . . .
Have you seen my pipe anywhere?
I'm sorry, not now . . .
Six . . . Five . . . Four . . . Three . . . Two . . .
One! . . . ZERO!
Observatory to Control Room . . . The nuclear motor has just taken over . . . All going well. Cut the auxiliary engine.
Have you seen my pipe?
?
?
Your pipe? What would I want with your pipe? . . . I'm sorry but I haven't time to worry about your pipe now!
Observatory to Control Room . . . How's the radar working?
Perfectly! All going well!
Meanwhile, many thousands of miles away . . .
Patience! We can't intervene for some hours yet . . .
Observatory to Control Room . . . Correction: zero . . . zero . . . eight . . . six . . . Please repeat.
Zero . . . zero . . . eight . . . six . . . Correction made . . .
A trifling correction, I think. But I'd better just check with my tables . . .
OH!
?

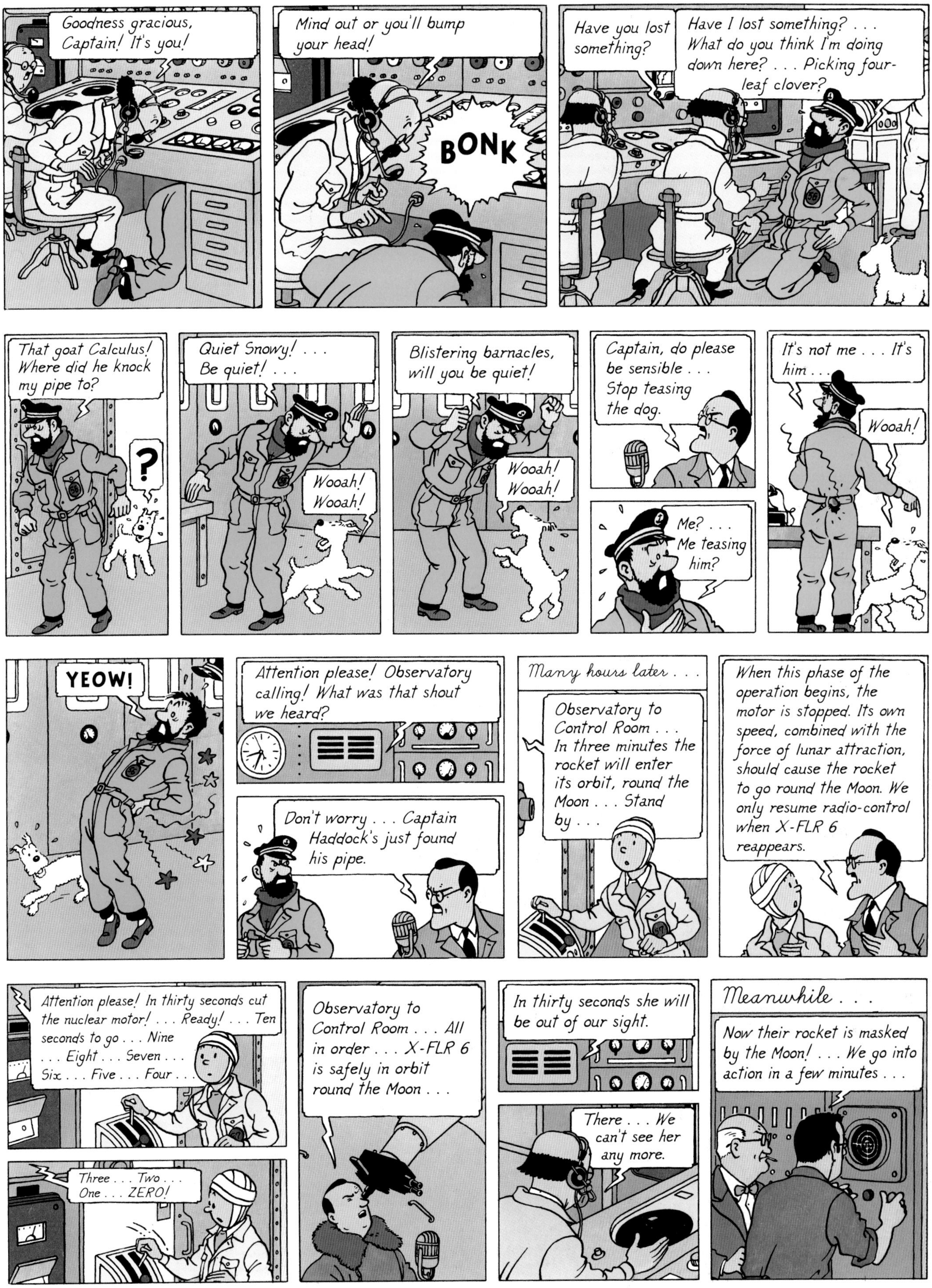
Goodness gracious, Captain! It's you!
Mind out or you'll bump your head!
BONK
Have you lost something?
Have I lost something? . . . What do you think I'm doing down here? . . . Picking four-leaf clover?
That goat Calculus! Where did he knock my pipe to?
?
Quiet Snowy! . . . Be quiet! . . .
Wooah! Wooah!
Blistering barnacles, will you be quiet!
Wooah! Wooah!
Captain, do please be sensible . . . Stop teasing the dog.
Me? . . . Me teasing him?
It's not me . . . It's him . . .
Wooah!
YEOW!
Attention please! Observatory calling! What was that shout we heard?
Don't worry . . . Captain Haddock's just found his pipe.
Many hours later . . .
Observatory to Control Room . . . In three minutes the rocket will enter its orbit, round the Moon . . . Stand by . . .
When this phase of the operation begins, the motor is stopped. Its own speed, combined with the force of lunar attraction, should cause the rocket to go round the Moon. We only resume radio-control when X-FLR 6 reappears.
Attention please! In thirty seconds cut the nuclear motor! . . . Ready! . . . Ten seconds to go . . . Nine . . . Eight . . . Seven . . . Six . . . Five . . . Four . . .
Three . . . Two . . . One . . . ZERO!
Observatory to Control Room . . . All in order . . . X-FLR 6 is safely in orbit round the Moon . . .
In thirty seconds she will be out of our sight.
There . . . We can't see her any more.
Meanwhile . . .
Now their rocket is masked by the Moon! . . . We go into action in a few minutes . . .

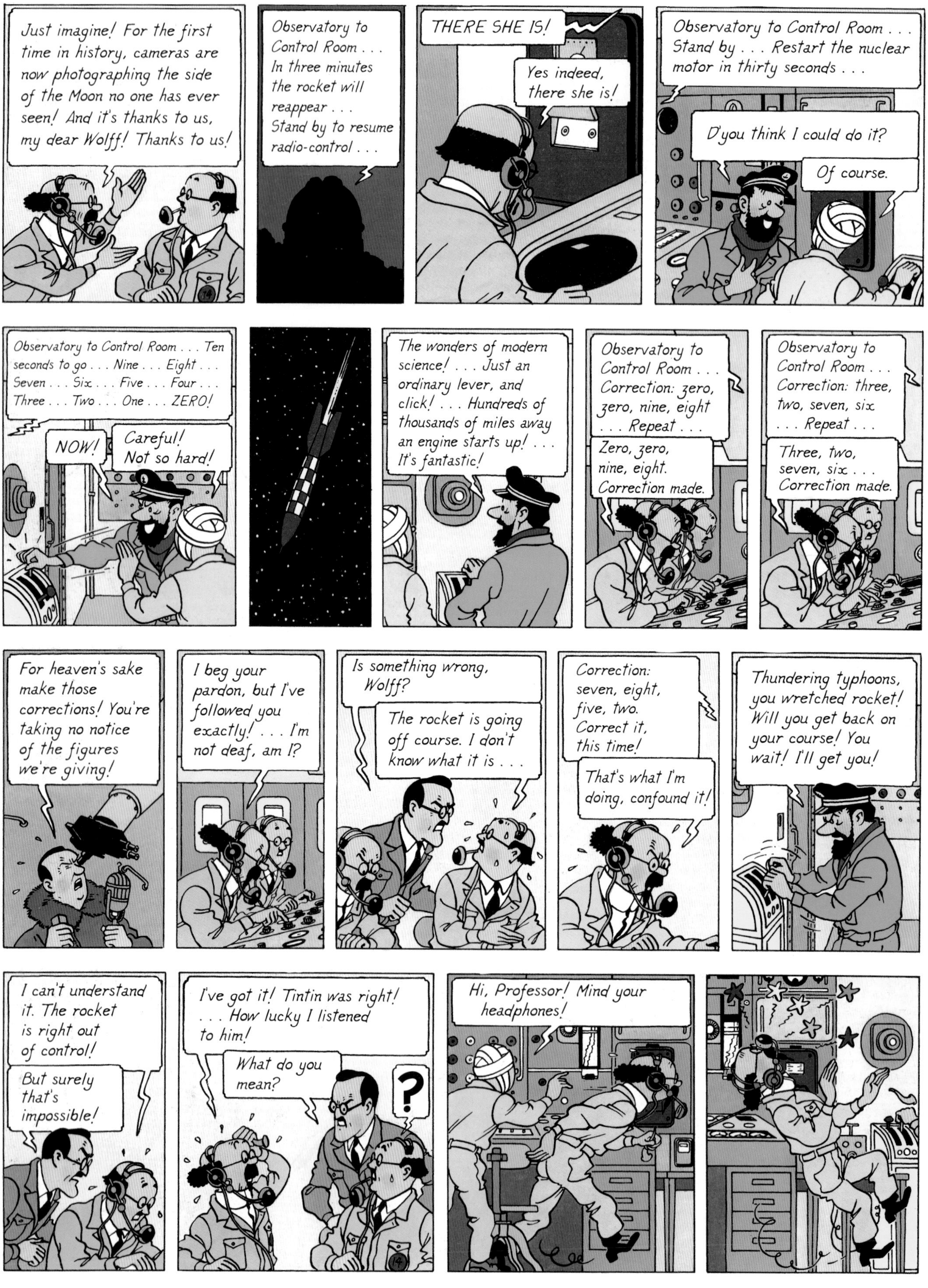

Just imagine! For the first time in history, cameras are now photographing the side of the Moon no one has ever seen! And it's thanks to us, my dear Wolff! Thanks to us!
Observatory to Control Room . . . In three minutes the rocket will reappear . . . Stand by to resume radio-control . . .
THERE SHE IS!
Yes indeed, there she is!
Observatory to Control Room . . . Stand by . . . Restart the nuclear motor in thirty seconds . . .
D'you think I could do it?
Of course.
Observatory to Control Room . . . Ten seconds to go . . . Nine . . . Eight . . . Seven . . . Six . . . Five . . . Four . . . Three . . . Two . . . One . . . ZERO!
NOW!
Careful! Not so hard!
The wonders of modern science! . . . Just an ordinary lever, and click! . . . Hundreds of thousands of miles away an engine starts up! . . . It's fantastic!
Observatory to Control Room . . . Correction: zero, zero, nine, eight . . . Repeat . . .
Zero, zero, nine, eight. Correction made.
Observatory to Control Room . . . Correction: three, two, seven, six . . . Repeat . . .
Three, two, seven, six . . . Correction made.
For heaven's sake make those corrections! You're taking no notice of the figures we're giving!
I beg your pardon, but I've followed you exactly! . . . I'm not deaf, am I?
Is something wrong, Wolff?
The rocket is going off course. I don't know what it is . . .
Correction: seven, eight, five, two. Correct it, this time!
That's what I'm doing, confound it!
Thundering typhoons, you wretched rocket! Will you get back on your course! You wait! I'll get you!
I can't understand it. The rocket is right out of control!
But surely that's impossible!
I've got it! Tintin was right! . . . How lucky I listened to him!
What do you mean?
?
Hi, Professor! Mind your headphones!

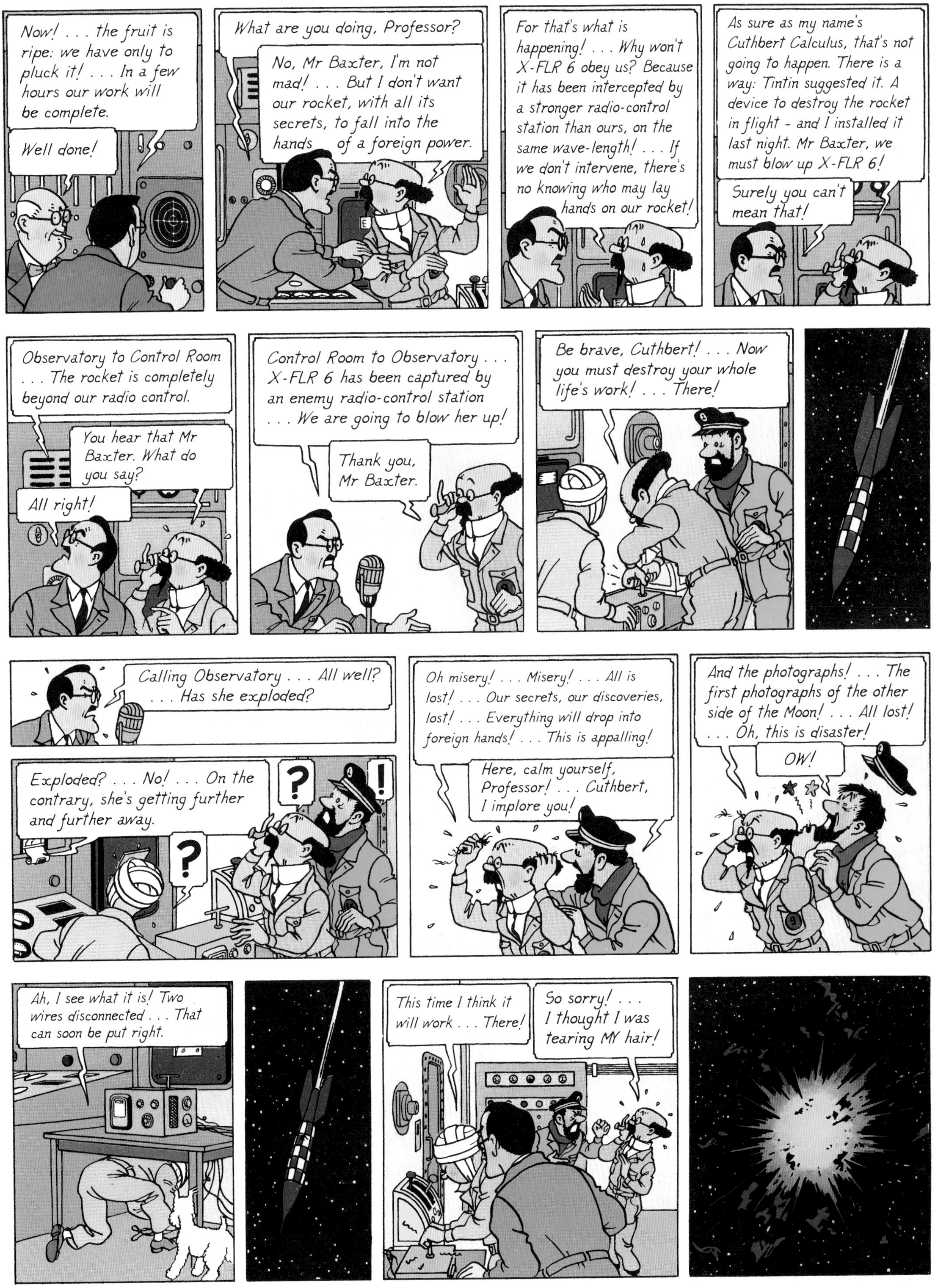
Now! . . . the fruit is ripe: we have only to pluck it! . . . In a few hours our work will be complete.
Well done!
What are you doing, Professor?
No, Mr Baxter, I'm not mad! . . . But I don't want our rocket, with all its secrets, to fall into the hands of a foreign power.
For that's what is happening! . . . Why won't X-FLR 6 obey us? Because it has been intercepted by a stronger radio-control station than ours, on the same wave-length! . . . If we don't intervene, there's no knowing who may lay hands on our rocket!
As sure as my name's Cuthbert Calculus, that's not going to happen. There is a way: Tintin suggested it. A device to destroy the rocket in flight - and I installed it last night. Mr Baxter, we must blow up X-FLR 6!
Surely you can't mean that!
Observatory to Control Room . . . The rocket is completely beyond our radio control.
You hear that Mr Baxter. What do you say?
All right!
Control Room to Observatory . . . X-FLR 6 has been captured by an enemy radio-control station . . . We are going to blow her up!
Thank you, Mr Baxter.
Be brave, Cuthbert! . . . Now you must destroy your whole life's work! . . . There!
Calling Observatory . . . All well? . . . Has she exploded?
Exploded? . . . No! . . . On the contrary, she's getting further and further away.
?
!
?
Oh misery! . . . Misery! . . . All is lost! . . . Our secrets, our discoveries, lost! . . . Everything will drop into foreign hands! . . . This is appalling!
Here, calm yourself, Professor! . . . Cuthbert, I implore you!
And the photographs! . . . The first photographs of the other side of the Moon! . . . All lost! . . . Oh, this is disaster!
OW!
Ah, I see what it is! Two wires disconnected . . . That can soon be put right.
This time I think it will work . . . There!
So sorry! . . . I thought I was tearing MY hair!

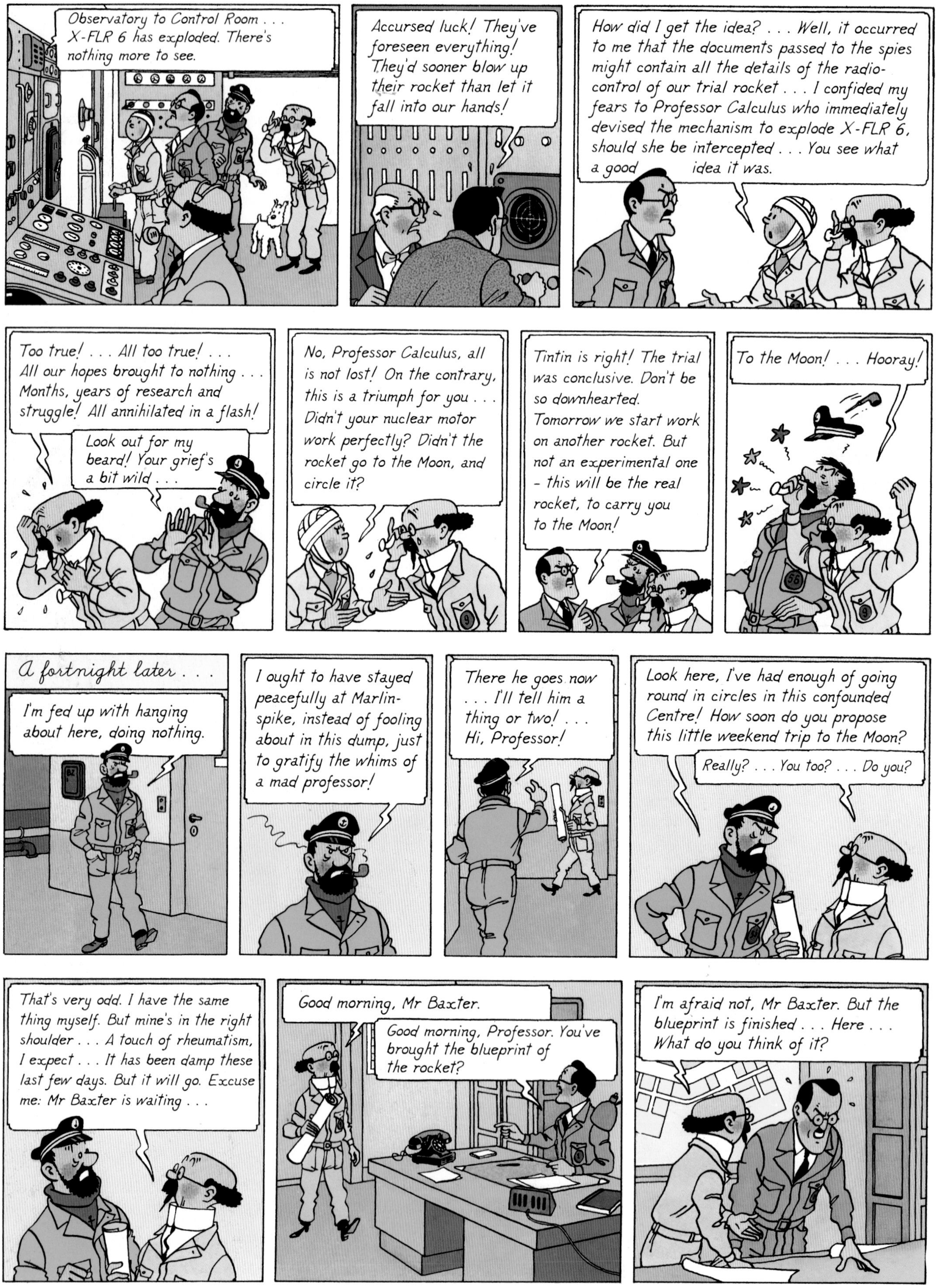
Observatory to Control Room . . . X-FLR 6 has exploded. There's nothing more to see.
Accursed luck! They've foreseen everything! They'd sooner blow up their rocket than let it fall into our hands!
How did I get the idea? . . . Well, it occurred to me that the documents passed to the spies might contain all the details of the radio-control of our trial rocket . . . I confided my fears to Professor Calculus who immediately devised the mechanism to explode X-FLR 6, should she be intercepted . . . You see what a good idea it was.
Too true! . . . All too true! . . . All our hopes brought to nothing . . . Months, years of research and struggle! All annihilated in a flash!
Look out for my beard! Your grief's a bit wild . . .
No, Professor Calculus, all is not lost! On the contrary, this is a triumph for you . . . Didn't your nuclear motor work perfectly? Didn't the rocket go to the Moon, and circle it?
Tintin is right! The trial was conclusive. Don't be so downhearted. Tomorrow we start work on another rocket. But not an experimental one - this will be the real rocket, to carry you to the Moon!
To the Moon! . . . Hooray!
A fortnight later . . .
I'm fed up with hanging about here, doing nothing.
I ought to have stayed peacefully at Marlinspike, instead of fooling about in this dump, just to gratify the whims of a mad professor!
There he goes now . . . I'll tell him a thing or two! . . . Hi, Professor!
Look here, I've had enough of going round in circles in this confounded Centre! How soon do you propose this little weekend trip to the Moon?
Really? . . . You too? . . . Do you?
That's very odd. I have the same thing myself. But mine's in the right shoulder . . . A touch of rheumatism, I expect . . . It has been damp these last few days. But it will go. Excuse me: Mr Baxter is waiting . . .
Good morning, Mr Baxter.
Good morning, Professor. You've brought the blueprint of the rocket?
I'm afraid not, Mr Baxter. But the blueprint is finished . . . Here . . . What do you think of it?

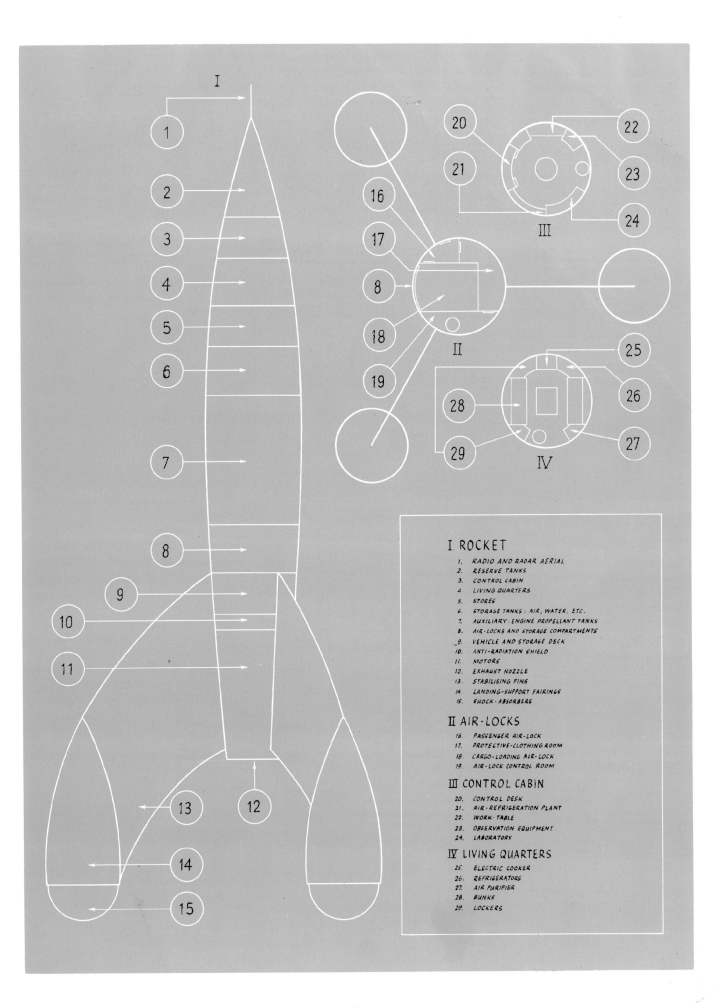

I. ROCKET

1. RADIO AND RADAR AERIAL
2. RESERVE TANKS
3. CONTROL CABIN
4. LIVING QUARTERS
5. STORES
6. STORAGE TANKS : AIR, WATER, ETC.
7. AUXILIARY-ENGINE PROPELLANT TANKS
8. AIR-LOCKS AND STORAGE COMPARTMENTS
9. VEHICLE AND STORAGE DECK
10. ANTI-RADIATION SHIELD
11. MOTORS
12. EXHAUST NOZZLE
13. STABILISING FINS
14. LANDING-SUPPORT FAIRINGS
15. SHOCK-ABSORBERS

II AIR-LOCKS

16. PASSENGER AIR-LOCK
17. PROTECTIVE-CLOTHING ROOM
18. CARGO-LOADING AIR-LOCK
19. AIR-LOCK CONTROL ROOM

III CONTROL CABIN

20. CONTROL DESK
21. AIR-REFRIGERATION PLANT
22. WORK-TABLE
23. OBSERVATION EQUIPMENT
24. LABORATORY

IV LIVING QUARTERS

25. ELECTRIC COOKER
26. REFRIGERATORS
27. AIR PURIFIER
28. BUNKS
29. LOCKERS

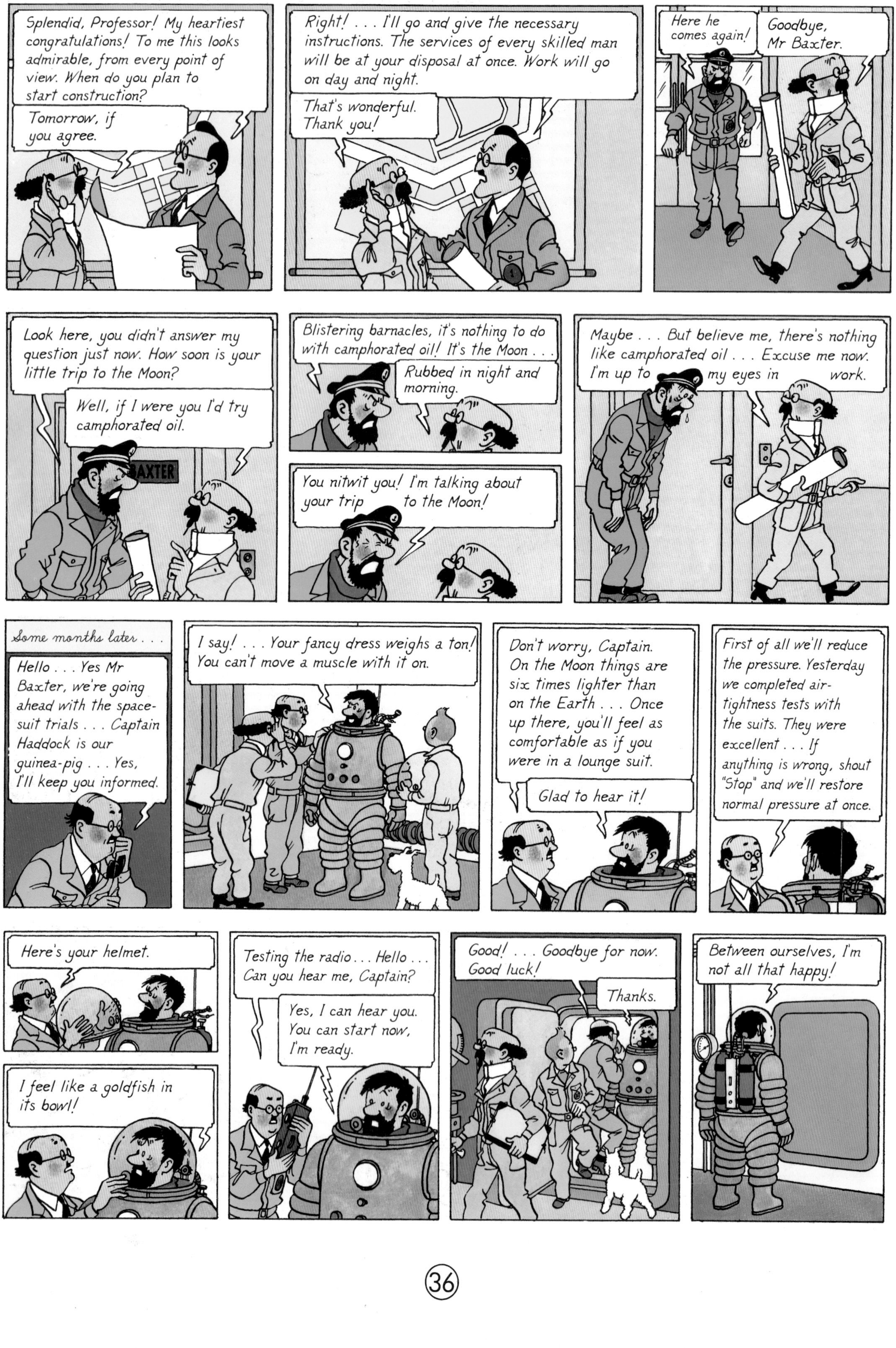

Splendid, Professor! My heartiest congratulations! To me this looks admirable, from every point of view. When do you plan to start construction?
Tomorrow, if you agree.
Right! . . . I'll go and give the necessary instructions. The services of every skilled man will be at your disposal at once. Work will go on day and night.
That's wonderful. Thank you!
Here he comes again!
Goodbye, Mr Baxter.
Look here, you didn't answer my question just now. How soon is your little trip to the Moon?
Well, if I were you I'd try camphorated oil.
BAXTER
Blistering barnacles, it's nothing to do with camphorated oil! It's the Moon . . .
Rubbed in night and morning.
You nitwit you! I'm talking about your trip to the Moon!
Maybe . . . But believe me, there's nothing like camphorated oil . . . Excuse me now. I'm up to my eyes in work.
Some months later . . .
Hello . . . Yes Mr Baxter, we're going ahead with the space-suit trials . . . Captain Haddock is our guinea-pig . . . Yes, I'll keep you informed.
I say! . . . Your fancy dress weighs a ton! You can't move a muscle with it on.
Don't worry, Captain. On the Moon things are six times lighter than on the Earth . . . Once up there, you'll feel as comfortable as if you were in a lounge suit.
Glad to hear it!
First of all we'll reduce the pressure. Yesterday we completed air-tightness tests with the suits. They were excellent . . . If anything is wrong, shout "Stop" and we'll restore normal pressure at once.
Here's your helmet.
I feel like a goldfish in its bowl!
Testing the radio . . . Hello . . . Can you hear me, Captain?
Yes, I can hear you. You can start now, I'm ready.
Good! . . . Goodbye for now. Good luck!
Thanks.
Between ourselves, I'm not all that happy!

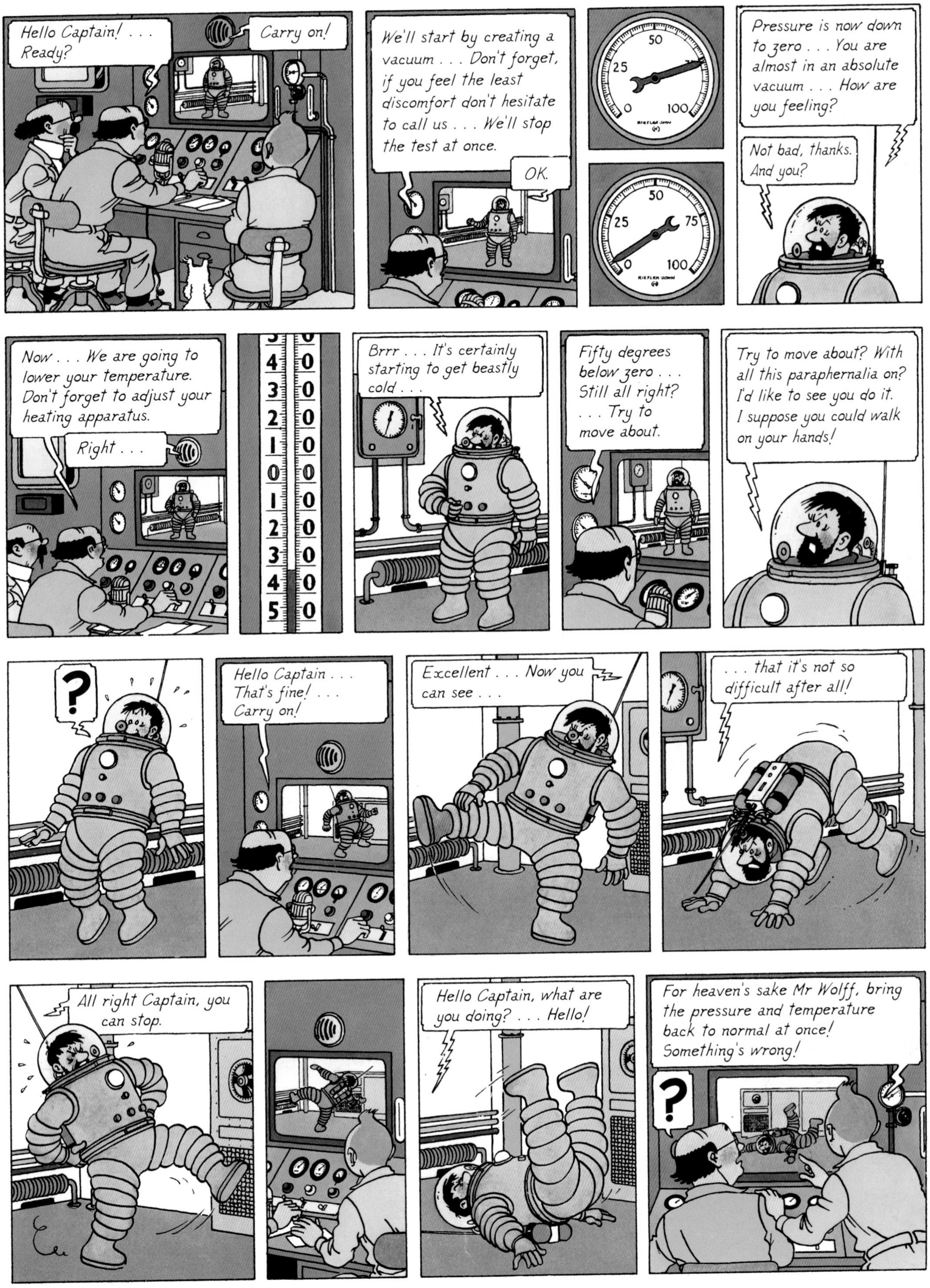

Hello Captain! . . . Ready?
Carry on!
We'll start by creating a vacuum . . . Don't forget, if you feel the least discomfort don't hesitate to call us . . . We'll stop the test at once.
OK.
50
25
0
100
50
25
75
0
100
Pressure is now down to zero . . . You are almost in an absolute vacuum . . . How are you feeling?
Not bad, thanks. And you?
Now . . . We are going to lower your temperature. Don't forget to adjust your heating apparatus.
Right . . .
Brrr . . . It's certainly starting to get beastly cold . . .
Fifty degrees below zero . . . Still all right? . . . Try to move about.
Try to move about? With all this paraphernalia on? I'd like to see you do it. I suppose you could walk on your hands!
?
Hello Captain . . . That's fine! . . . Carry on!
Excellent . . . Now you can see . . .
. . . that it's not so difficult after all!
All right Captain, you can stop.
Hello Captain, what are you doing? . . . Hello!
For heaven's sake Mr Wolff, bring the pressure and temperature back to normal at once! Something's wrong!
?

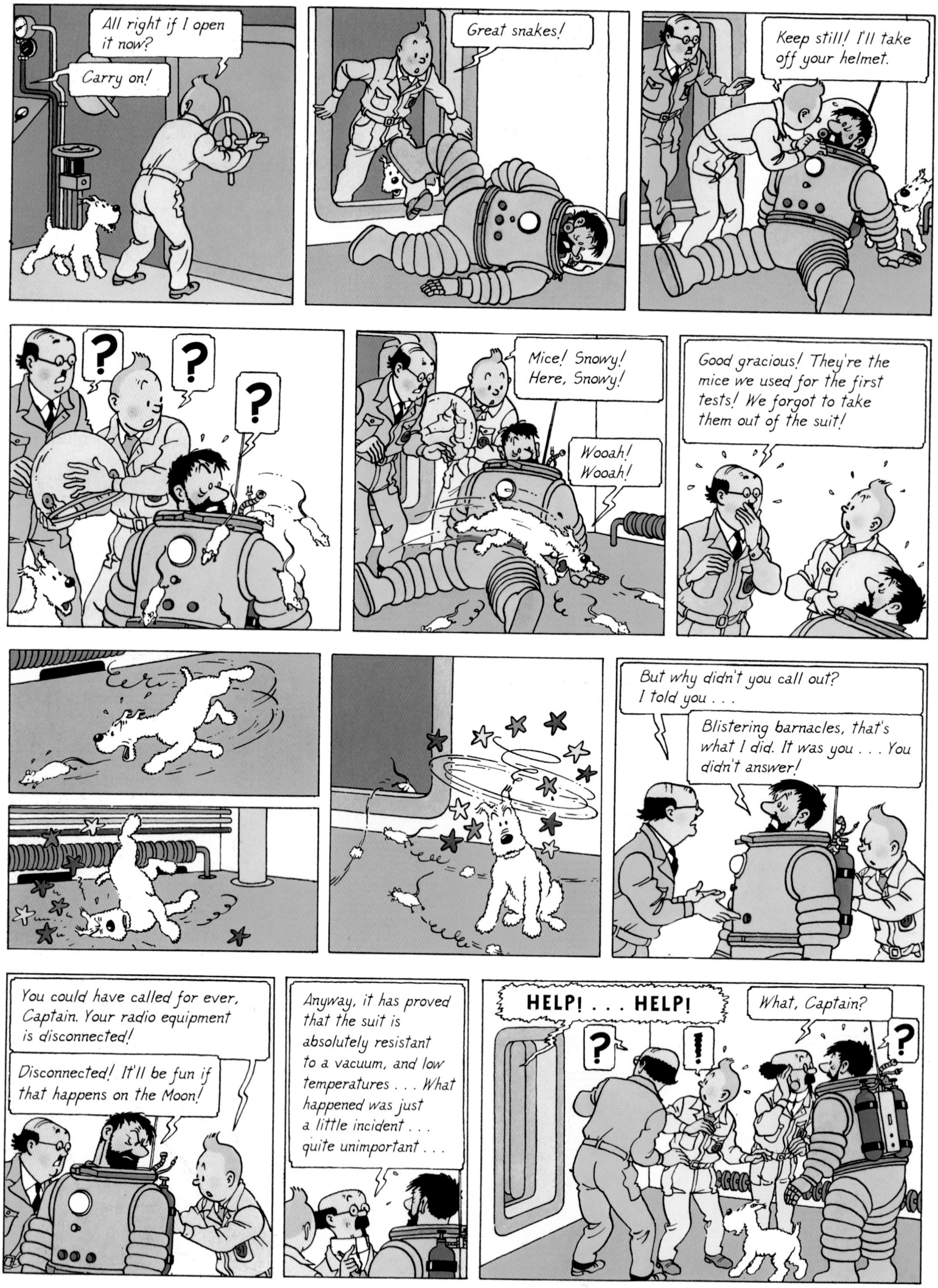
All right if I open it now?
Carry on!
Great snakes!
Keep still! I'll take off your helmet.
?
?
?
Mice! Snowy! Here, Snowy!
Wooah! Wooah!
Good gracious! They're the mice we used for the first tests! We forgot to take them out of the suit!
But why didn't you call out? I told you . . .
Blistering barnacles, that's what I did. It was you . . . You didn't answer!
You could have called for ever, Captain. Your radio equipment is disconnected!
Disconnected! It'll be fun if that happens on the Moon!
Anyway, it has proved that the suit is absolutely resistant to a vacuum, and low temperatures . . . What happened was just a little incident . . . quite unimportant . . .
HELP! . . . HELP!
?
!
What, Captain?
?

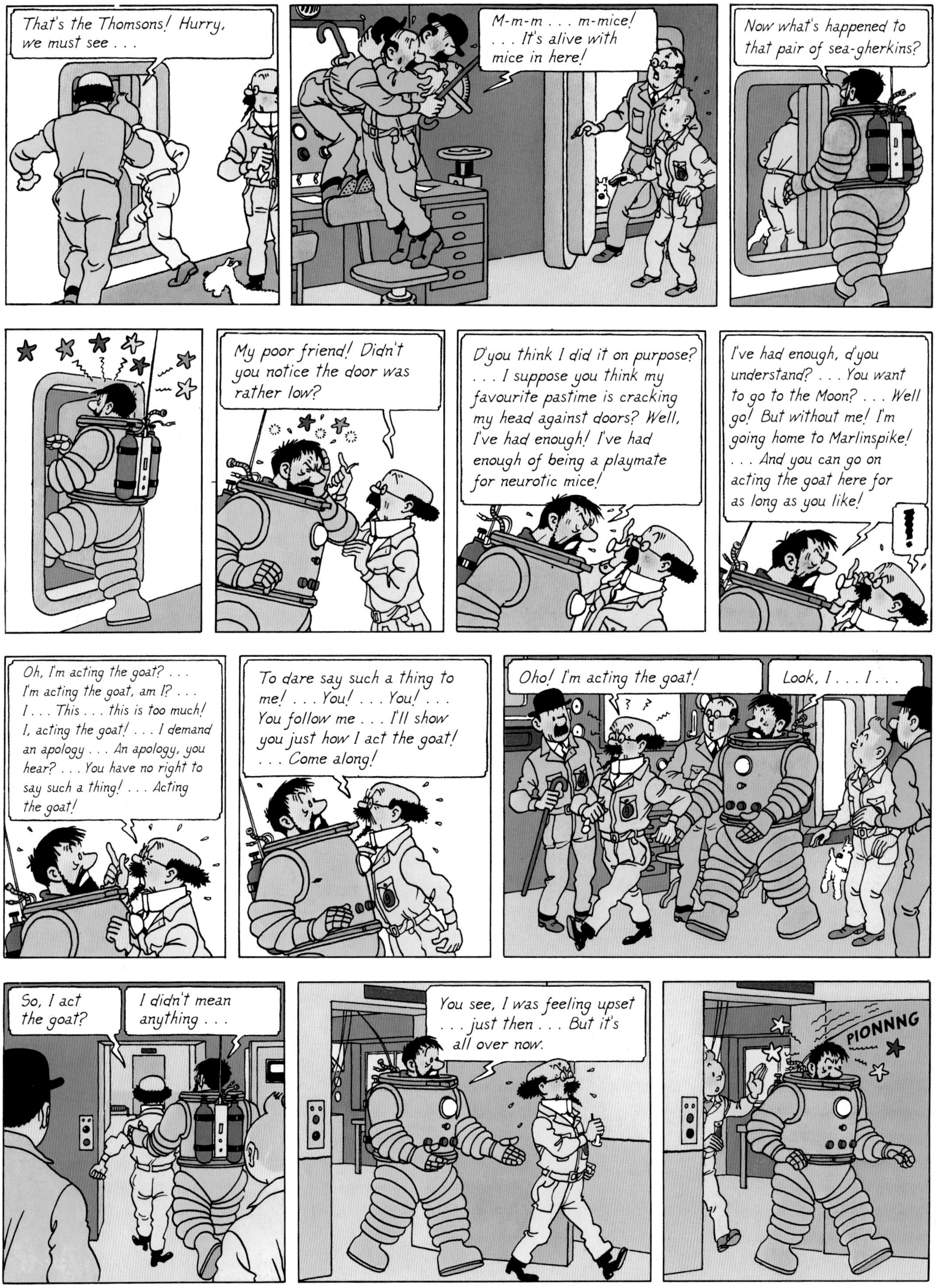

That's the Thomsons! Hurry, we must see . . .
M-m-m . . . m-mice! . . . It's alive with mice in here!
Now what's happened to that pair of sea-gherkins?
My poor friend! Didn't you notice the door was rather low?
D'you think I did it on purpose? . . . I suppose you think my favourite pastime is cracking my head against doors? Well, I've had enough! I've had enough of being a playmate for neurotic mice!
I've had enough, d'you understand? . . . You want to go to the Moon? . . . Well go! But without me! I'm going home to Marlinspike! . . . And you can go on acting the goat here for as long as you like!
!!!
Oh, I'm acting the goat? . . . I'm acting the goat, am I? . . . I . . . This . . . this is too much! I, acting the goat! . . . I demand an apology . . . An apology, you hear? . . . You have no right to say such a thing! . . . Acting the goat!
To dare say such a thing to me! . . . You! . . . You! . . . You follow me . . . I'll show you just how I act the goat! . . . Come along!
Oho! I'm acting the goat!
Look, I . . . I . . .
? ?
So, I act the goat?
I didn't mean anything . . .
You see, I was feeling upset . . . just then . . . But it's all over now.
PIONNNG

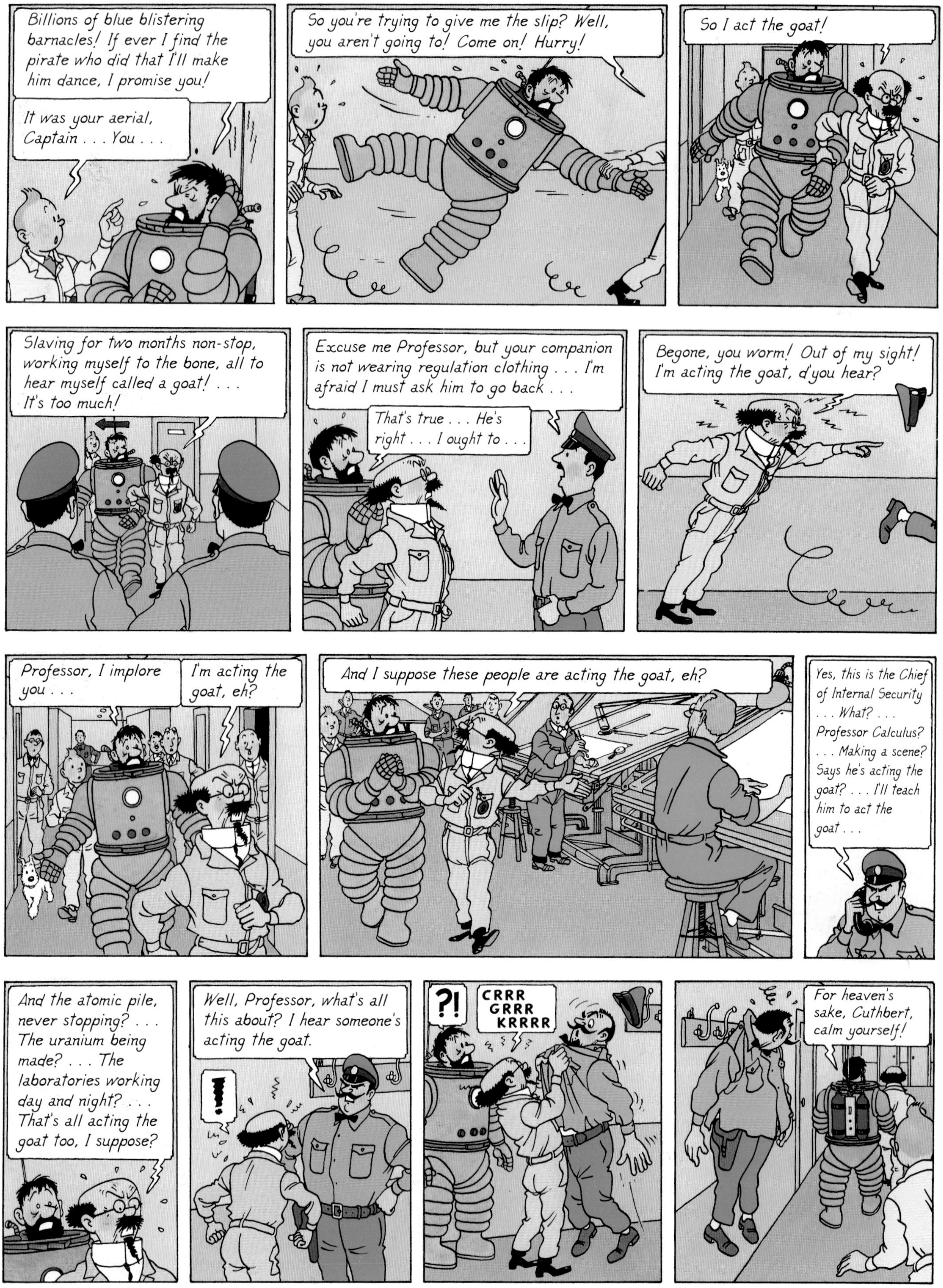
Billions of blue blistering barnacles! If ever I find the pirate who did that I'll make him dance, I promise you!
It was your aerial, Captain . . . You . . .
So you're trying to give me the slip? Well, you aren't going to! Come on! Hurry!
So I act the goat!
Slaving for two months non-stop, working myself to the bone, all to hear myself called a goat! . . . It's too much!
Excuse me Professor, but your companion is not wearing regulation clothing . . . I'm afraid I must ask him to go back . . .
That's true . . . He's right . . . I ought to . . .
Begone, you worm! Out of my sight! I'm acting the goat, d'you hear?
Professor, I implore you . . .
I'm acting the goat, eh?
And I suppose these people are acting the goat, eh?
Yes, this is the Chief of Internal Security . . . What? . . . Professor Calculus? . . . Making a scene? Says he's acting the goat? . . . I'll teach him to act the goat . . .
And the atomic pile, never stopping? . . . The uranium being made? . . . The laboratories working day and night? . . . That's all acting the goat too, I suppose?
Well, Professor, what's all this about? I hear someone's acting the goat.
!
?!
CRRR GRRR KRRRR
For heaven's sake, Cuthbert, calm yourself!

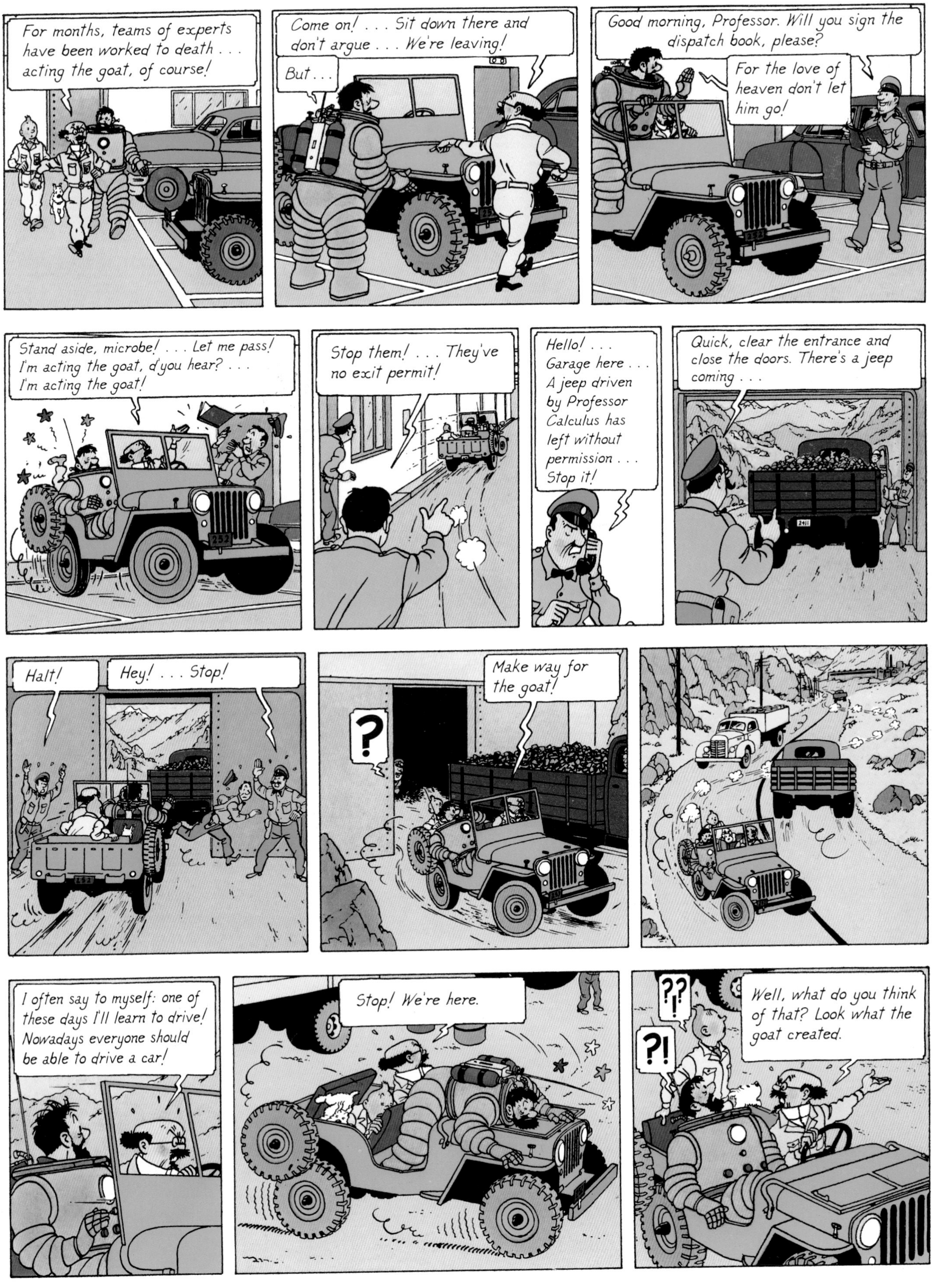
For months, teams of experts have been worked to death . . . acting the goat, of course!
Come on! . . . Sit down there and don't argue . . . We're leaving!
But . . .
Good morning, Professor. Will you sign the dispatch book, please?
For the love of heaven don't let him go!
Stand aside, microbe! . . . Let me pass! I'm acting the goat, d'you hear? . . . I'm acting the goat!
Stop them! . . . They've no exit permit!
Hello! . . . Garage here . . . A jeep driven by Professor Calculus has left without permission . . . Stop it!
Quick, clear the entrance and close the doors. There's a jeep coming . . .
Halt!
Hey! . . . Stop!
?
Make way for the goat!
I often say to myself: one of these days I'll learn to drive! Nowadays everyone should be able to drive a car!
Stop! We're here.
??!
?!
Well, what do you think of that? Look what the goat created.

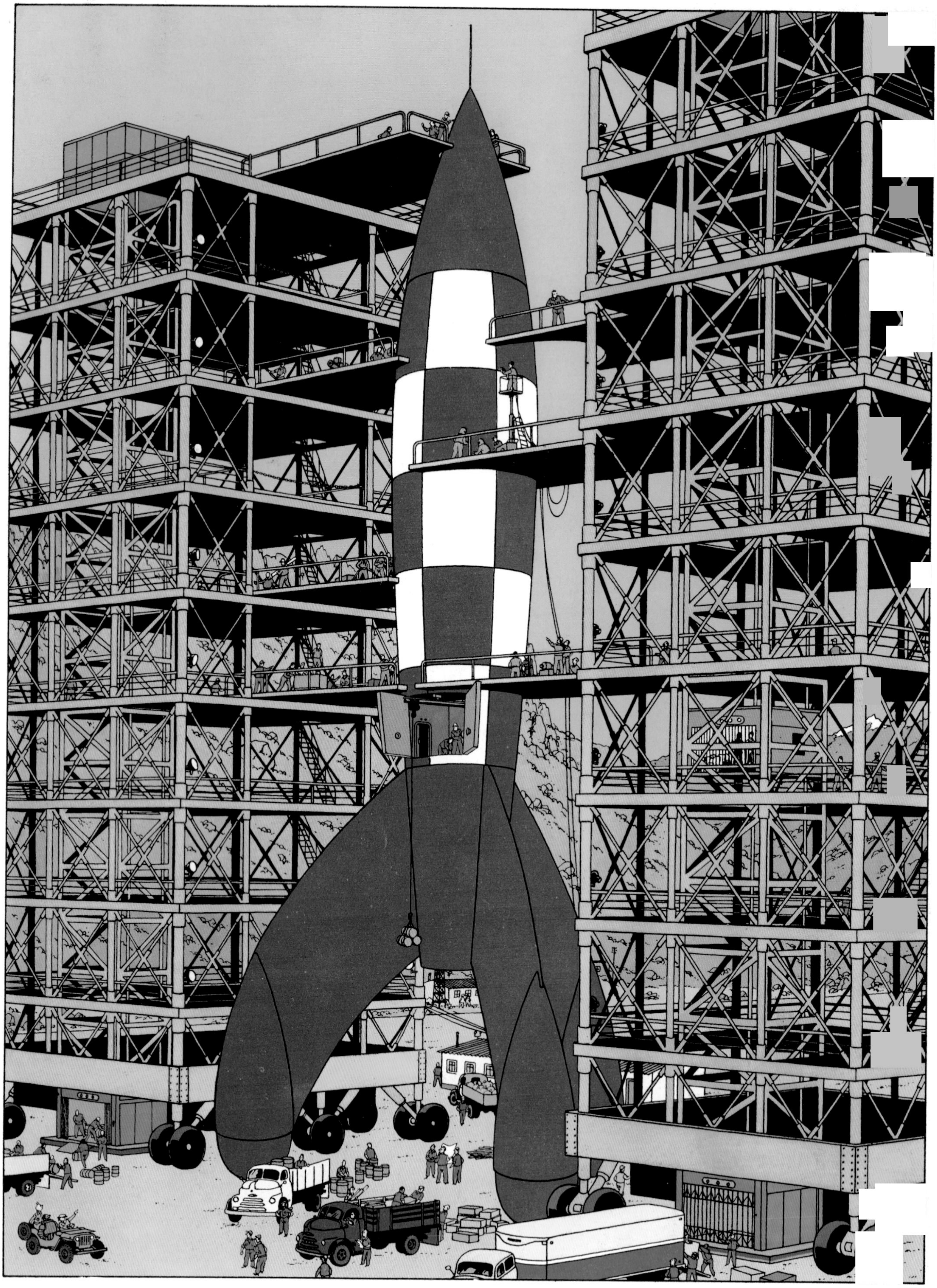

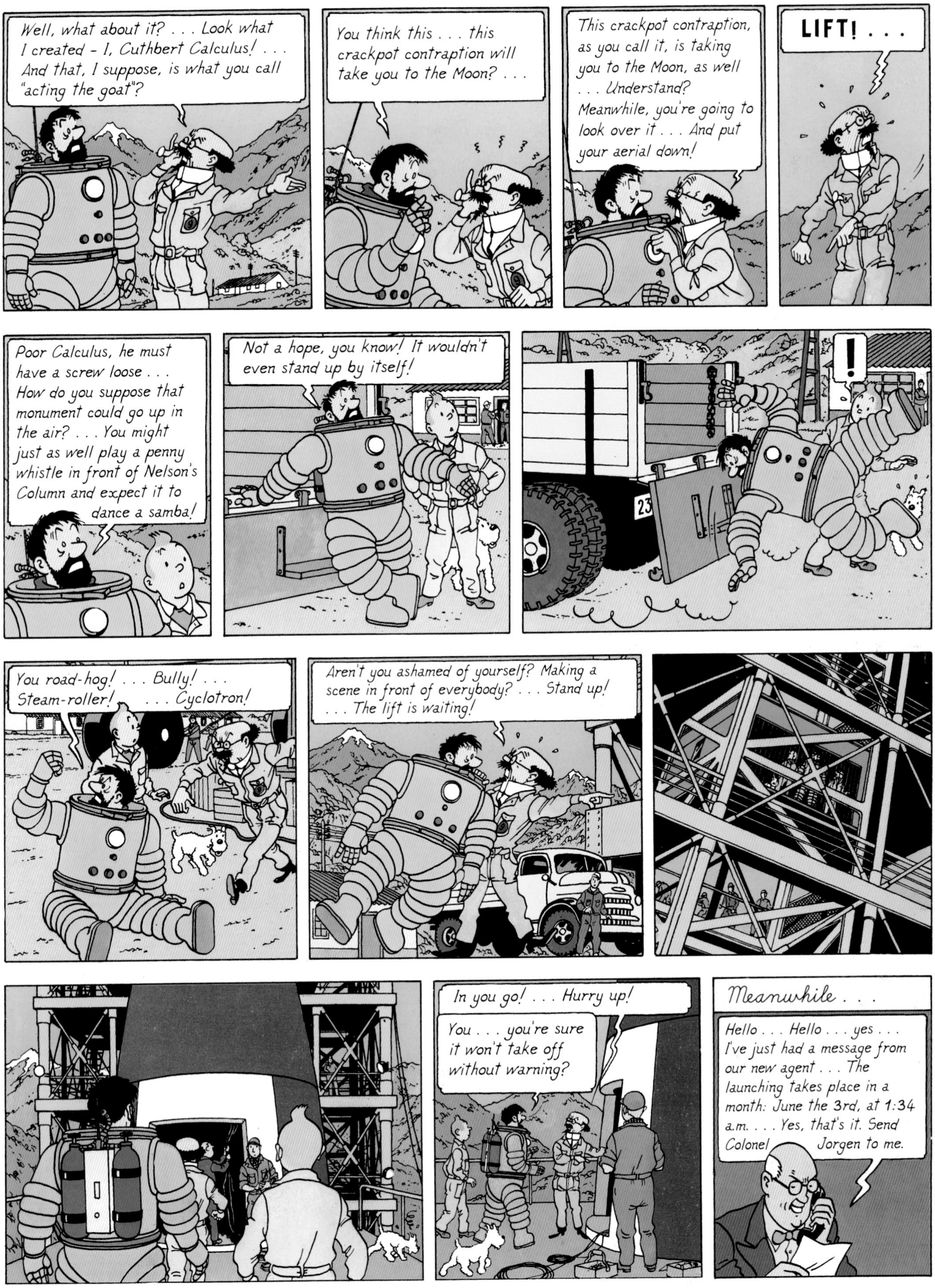
Well, what about it? . . . Look what I created - I, Cuthbert Calculus! . . . And that, I suppose, is what you call "acting the goat"?
You think this . . . this crackpot contraption will take you to the Moon? . . .
This crackpot contraption, as you call it, is taking you to the Moon, as well . . . Understand? Meanwhile, you're going to look over it . . . And put your aerial down!
LIFT! . . .
Poor Calculus, he must have a screw loose . . . How do you suppose that monument could go up in the air? . . . You might just as well play a penny whistle in front of Nelson's Column and expect it to dance a samba!
Not a hope, you know! It wouldn't even stand up by itself!
!
23
You road-hog! . . . Bully! . . . Steam-roller! . . . Cyclotron!
Aren't you ashamed of yourself? Making a scene in front of everybody? . . . Stand up! . . . The lift is waiting!
In you go! . . . Hurry up!
You . . . you're sure it won't take off without warning?
Meanwhile . . .
Hello . . . Hello . . . yes . . . I've just had a message from our new agent . . . The launching takes place in a month: June the 3rd, at 1:34 a.m. . . . Yes, that's it. Send Colonel Jorgen to me.

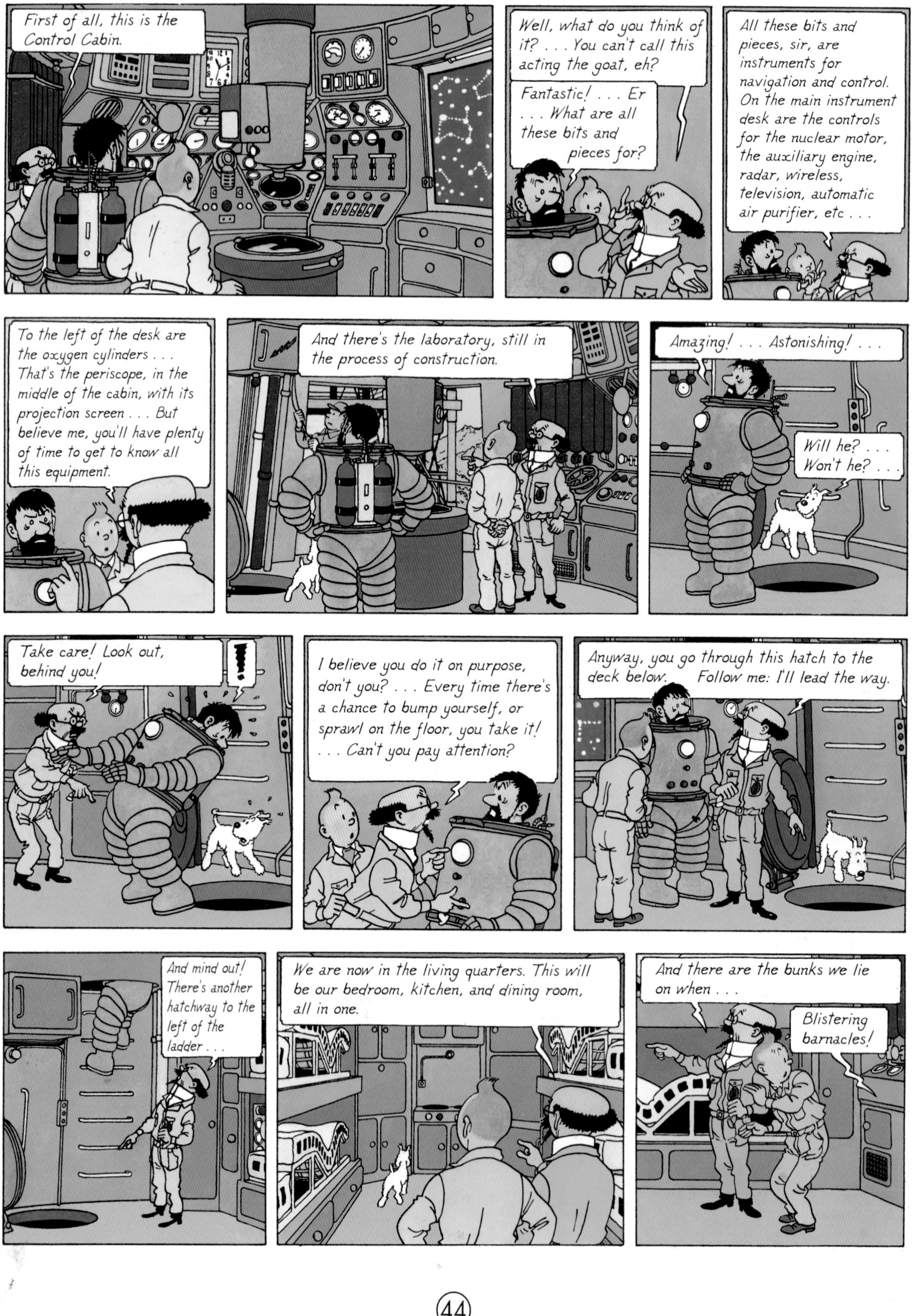
First of all, this is the Control Cabin.
Well, what do you think of it? . . . You can't call this acting the goat, eh?
Fantastic! . . . Er . . . What are all these bits and pieces for?
All these bits and pieces, sir, are instruments for navigation and control. On the main instrument desk are the controls for the nuclear motor, the auxiliary engine, radar, wireless, television, automatic air purifier, etc . . .
To the left of the desk are the oxygen cylinders . . . That's the periscope, in the middle of the cabin, with its projection screen . . . But believe me, you'll have plenty of time to get to know all this equipment.
And there's the laboratory, still in the process of construction.
Amazing! . . . Astonishing! . . .
Will he? . . . Won't he? . . .
Take care! Look out, behind you!
!
I believe you do it on purpose, don't you? . . . Every time there's a chance to bump yourself, or sprawl on the floor, you take it! . . . Can't you pay attention?
Anyway, you go through this hatch to the deck below. Follow me: I'll lead the way.
And mind out! There's another hatchway to the left of the ladder . . .
We are now in the living quarters. This will be our bedroom, kitchen, and dining room, all in one.
And there are the bunks we lie on when . . .
Blistering barnacles!

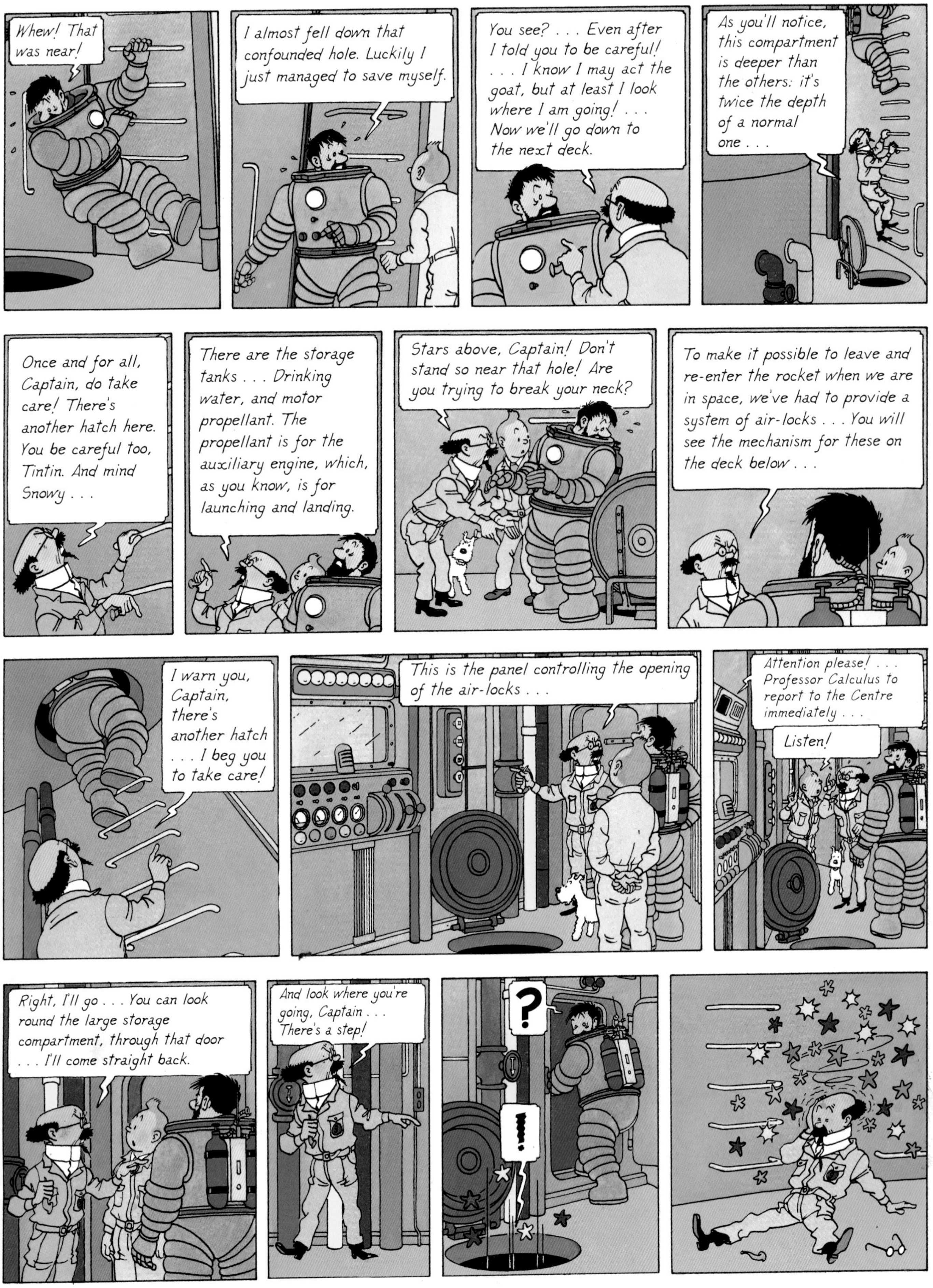
Whew! That was near!
I almost fell down that confounded hole. Luckily I just managed to save myself.
You see? . . . Even after I told you to be careful! . . . I know I may act the goat, but at least I look where I am going! . . . Now we'll go down to the next deck.
As you'll notice, this compartment is deeper than the others: it's twice the depth of a normal one . . .
Once and for all, Captain, do take care! There's another hatch here. You be careful too, Tintin. And mind Snowy . . .
There are the storage tanks . . . Drinking water, and motor propellant. The propellant is for the auxiliary engine, which, as you know, is for launching and landing.
Stars above, Captain! Don't stand so near that hole! Are you trying to break your neck?
To make it possible to leave and re-enter the rocket when we are in space, we've had to provide a system of air-locks . . . You will see the mechanism for these on the deck below . . .
I warn you, Captain, there's another hatch . . . I beg you to take care!
This is the panel controlling the opening of the air-locks . . .
Attention please! . . . Professor Calculus to report to the Centre immediately . . .
Listen!
Right, I'll go . . . You can look round the large storage compartment, through that door . . . I'll come straight back.
And look where you're going, Captain . . . There's a step!
?
!!!

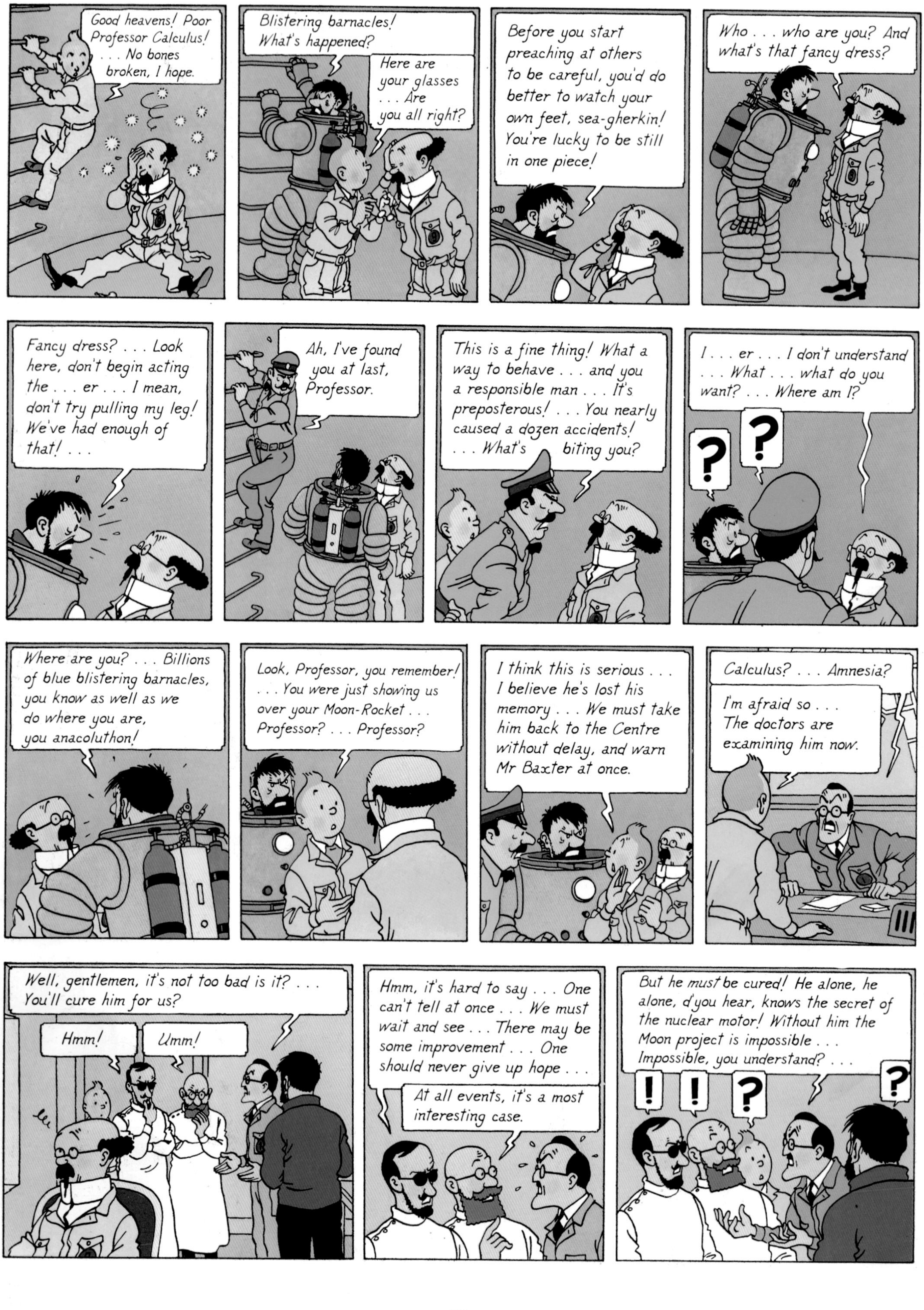
Good heavens! Poor Professor Calculus! . . . No bones broken, I hope.
Blistering barnacles! What's happened?
Here are your glasses . . . Are you all right?
Before you start preaching at others to be careful, you'd do better to watch your own feet, sea-gherkin! You're lucky to be still in one piece!
Who . . . who are you? And what's that fancy dress?
Fancy dress? . . . Look here, don't begin acting the . . . er . . . I mean, don't try pulling my leg! We've had enough of that! . . .
Ah, I've found you at last, Professor.
This is a fine thing! What a way to behave . . . and you a responsible man . . . It's preposterous! . . . You nearly caused a dozen accidents! . . . What's biting you?
I . . . er . . . I don't understand . . . What . . . what do you want? . . . Where am I?
?
?
Where are you? . . . Billions of blue blistering barnacles, you know as well as we do where you are, you anacoluthon!
Look, Professor, you remember! . . . You were just showing us over your Moon-Rocket . . . Professor? . . . Professor?
I think this is serious . . . I believe he's lost his memory . . . We must take him back to the Centre without delay, and warn Mr Baxter at once.
Calculus? . . . Amnesia?
I'm afraid so . . . The doctors are examining him now.
Well, gentlemen, it's not too bad is it? . . . You'll cure him for us?
Hmm!
Umm!
Hmm, it's hard to say . . . One can't tell at once . . . We must wait and see . . . There may be some improvement . . . One should never give up hope . . .
At all events, it's a most interesting case.
But he must be cured! He alone, he alone, d'you hear, knows the secret of the nuclear motor! Without him the Moon project is impossible . . . Impossible, you understand? . . .
!
!
?
?

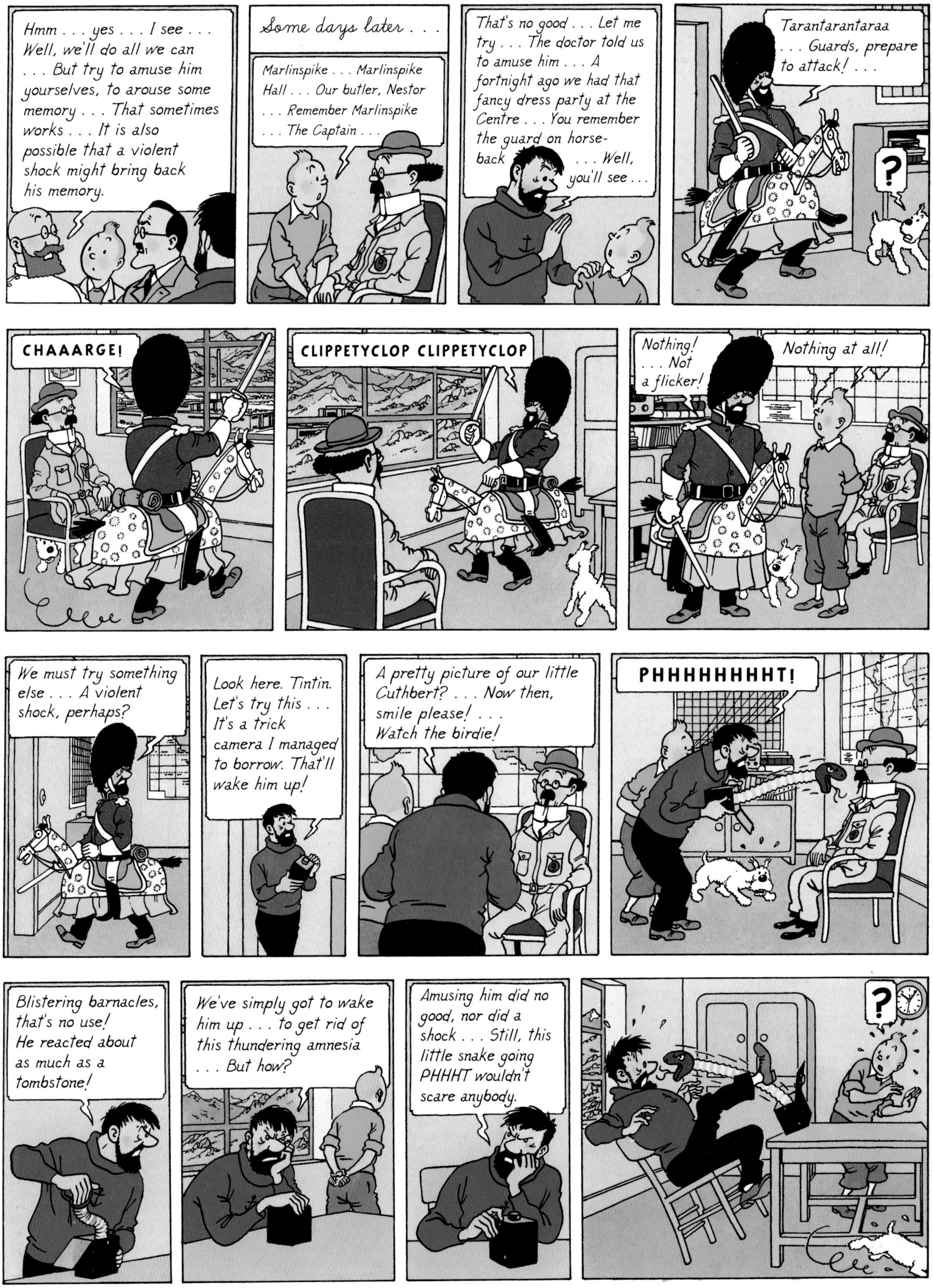

Hmm . . . yes . . . I see . . . Well, we'll do all we can . . . But try to amuse him yourselves, to arouse some memory . . . That sometimes works . . . It is also possible that a violent shock might bring back his memory.
Some days later . . .
Marlinspike . . . Marlinspike Hall . . . Our butler, Nestor . . . Remember Marlinspike . . . The Captain . . .
That's no good . . . Let me try . . . The doctor told us to amuse him . . . A fortnight ago we had that fancy dress party at the Centre . . . You remember the guard on horse-back . . . Well, you'll see . . .
Tarantarantaraa . . . Guards, prepare to attack! . . .
?
CHAAARGE!
CLIPPETYCLOP CLIPPETYCLOP
Nothing! . . . Not a flicker!
Nothing at all!
We must try something else . . . A violent shock, perhaps?
Look here. Tintin. Let's try this . . . It's a trick camera I managed to borrow. That'll wake him up!
A pretty picture of our little Cuthbert? . . . Now then, smile please! . . . Watch the birdie!
PHHHHHHHHT!
Blistering barnacles, that's no use! He reacted about as much as a tombstone!
We've simply got to wake him up . . . to get rid of this thundering amnesia . . . But how?
Amusing him did no good, nor did a shock . . . Still, this little snake going PHHHT wouldn't scare anybody.
?

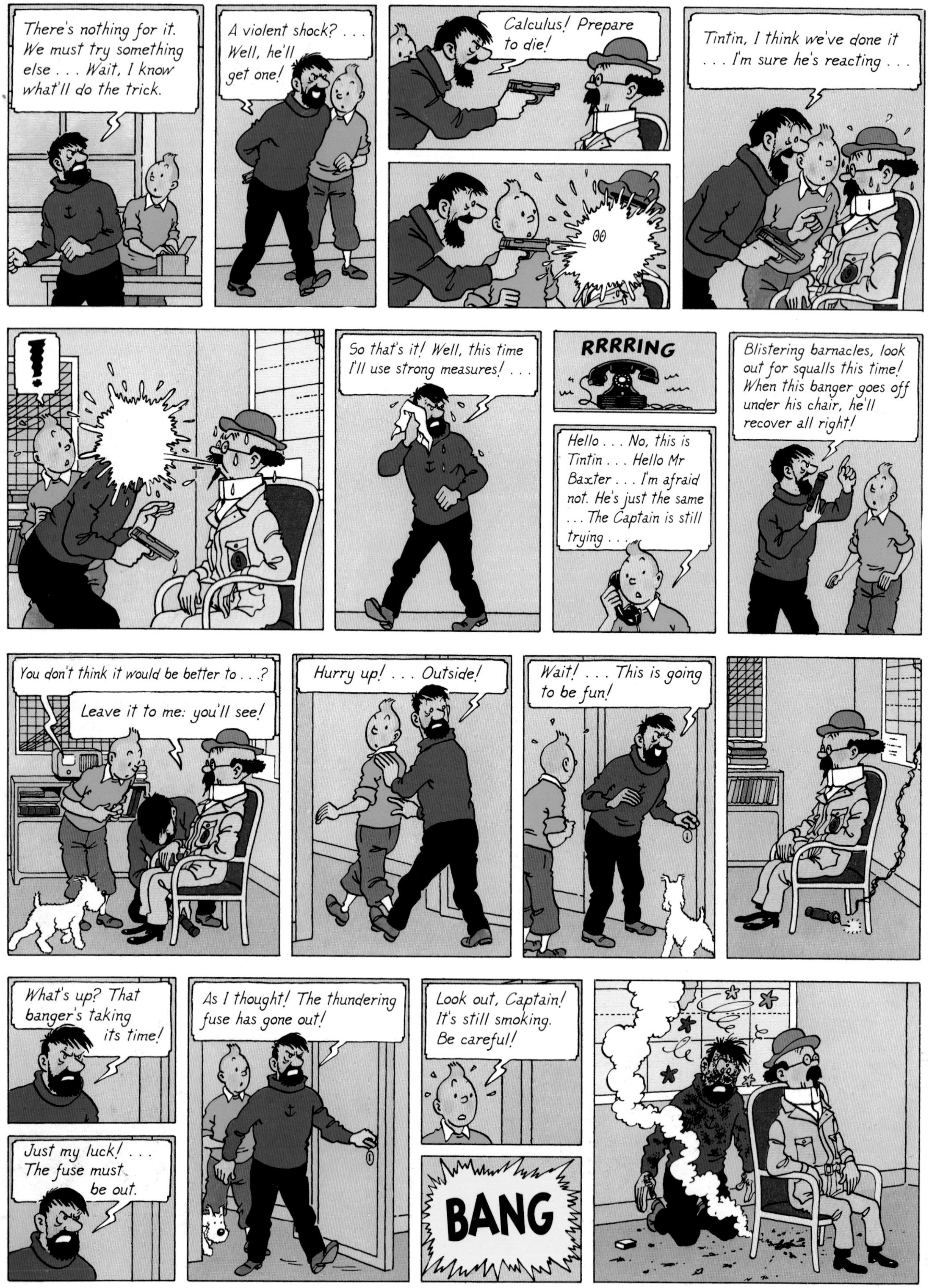
There's nothing for it. We must try something else . . . Wait, I know what'll do the trick.
A violent shock? . . . Well, he'll get one!
Calculus! Prepare to die!
Tintin, I think we've done it . . . I'm sure he's reacting . . .
So that's it! Well, this time I'll use strong measures! . . .
RRRRING
Hello . . . No, this is Tintin . . . Hello Mr Baxter . . . I'm afraid not. He's just the same . . . The Captain is still trying . . .
Blistering barnacles, look out for squalls this time! When this banger goes off under his chair, he'll recover all right!
You don't think it would be better to . . .?
Leave it to me: you'll see!
Hurry up! . . . Outside!
Wait! . . . This is going to be fun!
What's up? That banger's taking its time!
Just my luck! . . . The fuse must be out.
As I thought! The thundering fuse has gone out!
Look out, Captain! It's still smoking. Be careful!
BANG

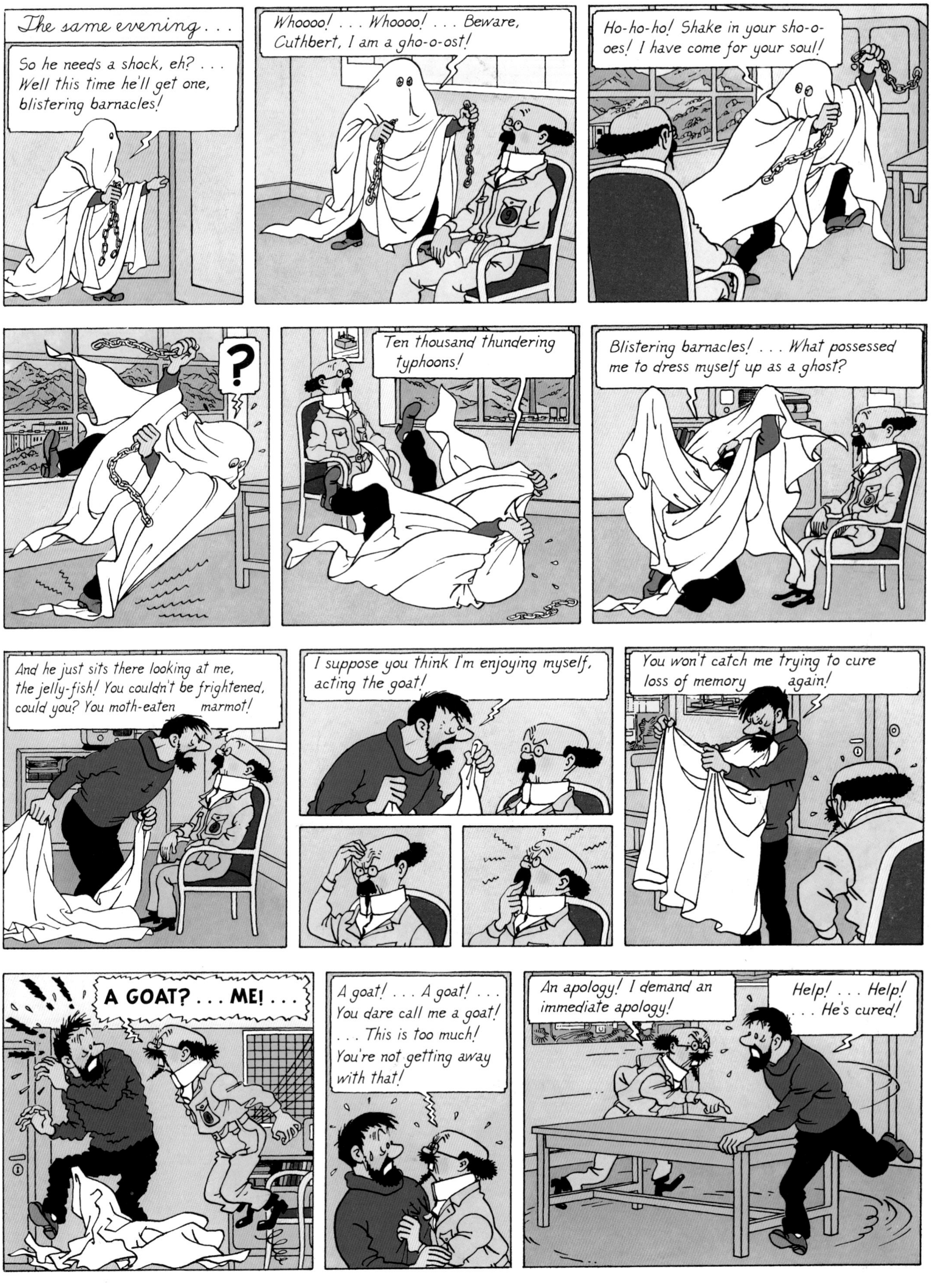
The same evening . . .
So he needs a shock, eh? . . . Well this time he'll get one, blistering barnacles!
Whoooo! . . . Whoooo! . . . Beware, Cuthbert, I am a gho-o-ost!
Ho-ho-ho! Shake in your sho-o-oes! I have come for your soul!
?
Ten thousand thundering typhoons!
Blistering barnacles! . . . What possessed me to dress myself up as a ghost?
And he just sits there looking at me, the jelly-fish! You couldn't be frightened, could you? You moth-eaten marmot!
I suppose you think I'm enjoying myself, acting the goat!
You won't catch me trying to cure loss of memory again!
A GOAT? . . . ME! . . .
A goat! . . . A goat! . . . You dare call me a goat! . . . This is too much! You're not getting away with that!
An apology! I demand an immediate apology!
Help! . . . Help! . . . He's cured!

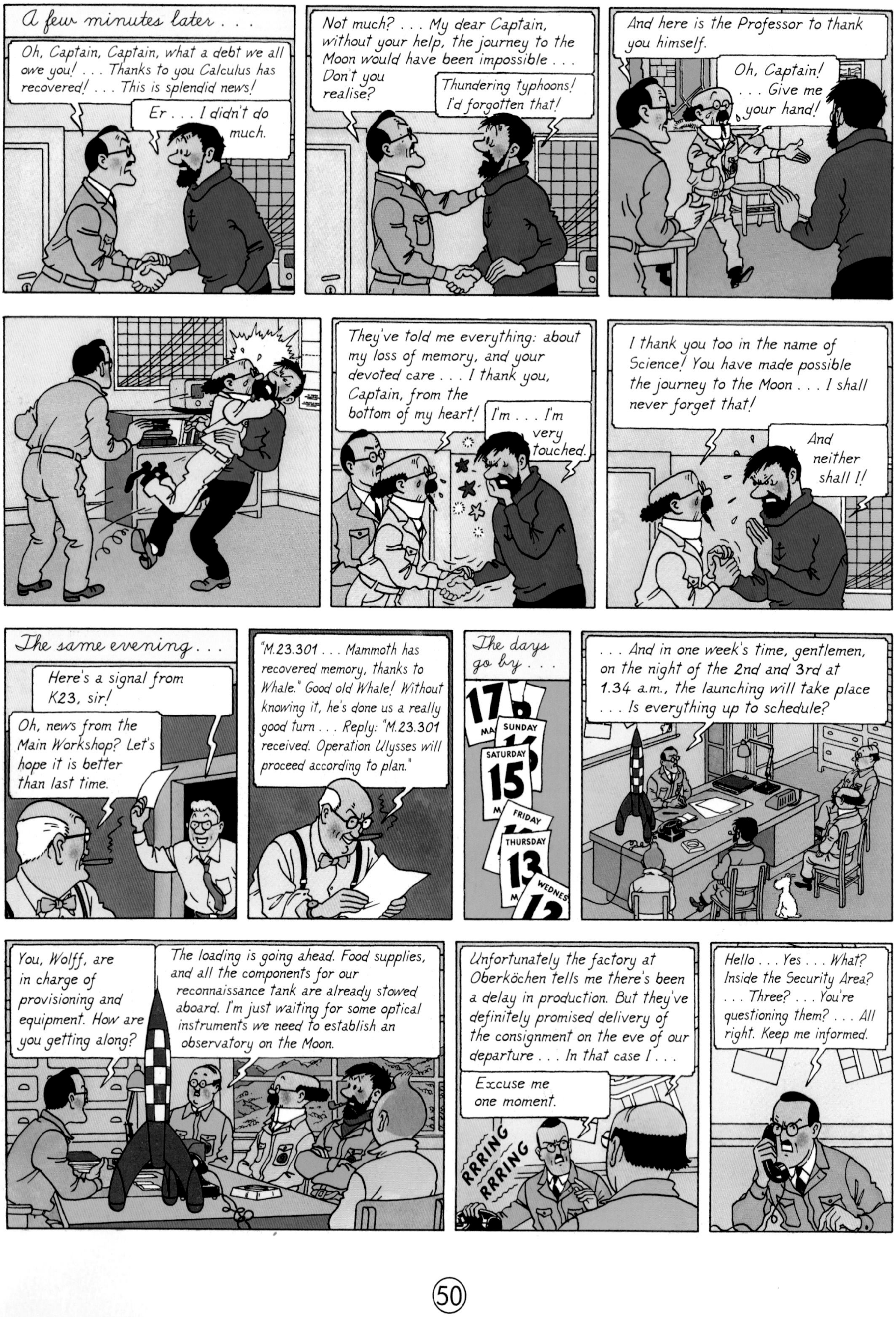
A few minutes later . . .
Oh, Captain, Captain, what a debt we all owe you! . . . Thanks to you Calculus has recovered! . . . This is splendid news!
Er . . . I didn't do much.
Not much? . . . My dear Captain, without your help, the journey to the Moon would have been impossible . . . Don't you realise?
Thundering typhoons! I'd forgotten that!
And here is the Professor to thank you himself.
Oh, Captain! . . . Give me your hand!
They've told me everything: about my loss of memory, and your devoted care . . . I thank you, Captain, from the bottom of my heart!
I'm . . . I'm very touched.
I thank you too in the name of Science! You have made possible the journey to the Moon . . . I shall never forget that!
And neither shall I!
The same evening . . .
Here's a signal from K23, sir!
Oh, news from the Main Workshop? Let's hope it is better than last time.
"M.23.301 . . . Mammoth has recovered memory, thanks to Whale." Good old Whale! Without knowing it, he's done us a really good turn . . . Reply: "M.23.301 received. Operation Ulysses will proceed according to plan."
The days go by . . .
SUNDAY
SATURDAY
15
FRIDAY
THURSDAY
13
. . . And in one week's time, gentlemen, on the night of the 2nd and 3rd at 1.34 a.m., the launching will take place . . . Is everything up to schedule?
You, Wolff, are in charge of provisioning and equipment. How are you getting along?
The loading is going ahead. Food supplies, and all the components for our reconnaissance tank are already stowed aboard. I'm just waiting for some optical instruments we need to establish an observatory on the Moon.
Unfortunately the factory at Oberköchen tells me there's been a delay in production. But they've definitely promised delivery of the consignment on the eve of our departure . . . In that case I . . .
Excuse me one moment.
RRRING
RRRING
Hello . . . Yes . . . What? Inside the Security Area? . . . Three? . . . You're questioning them? . . . All right. Keep me informed.

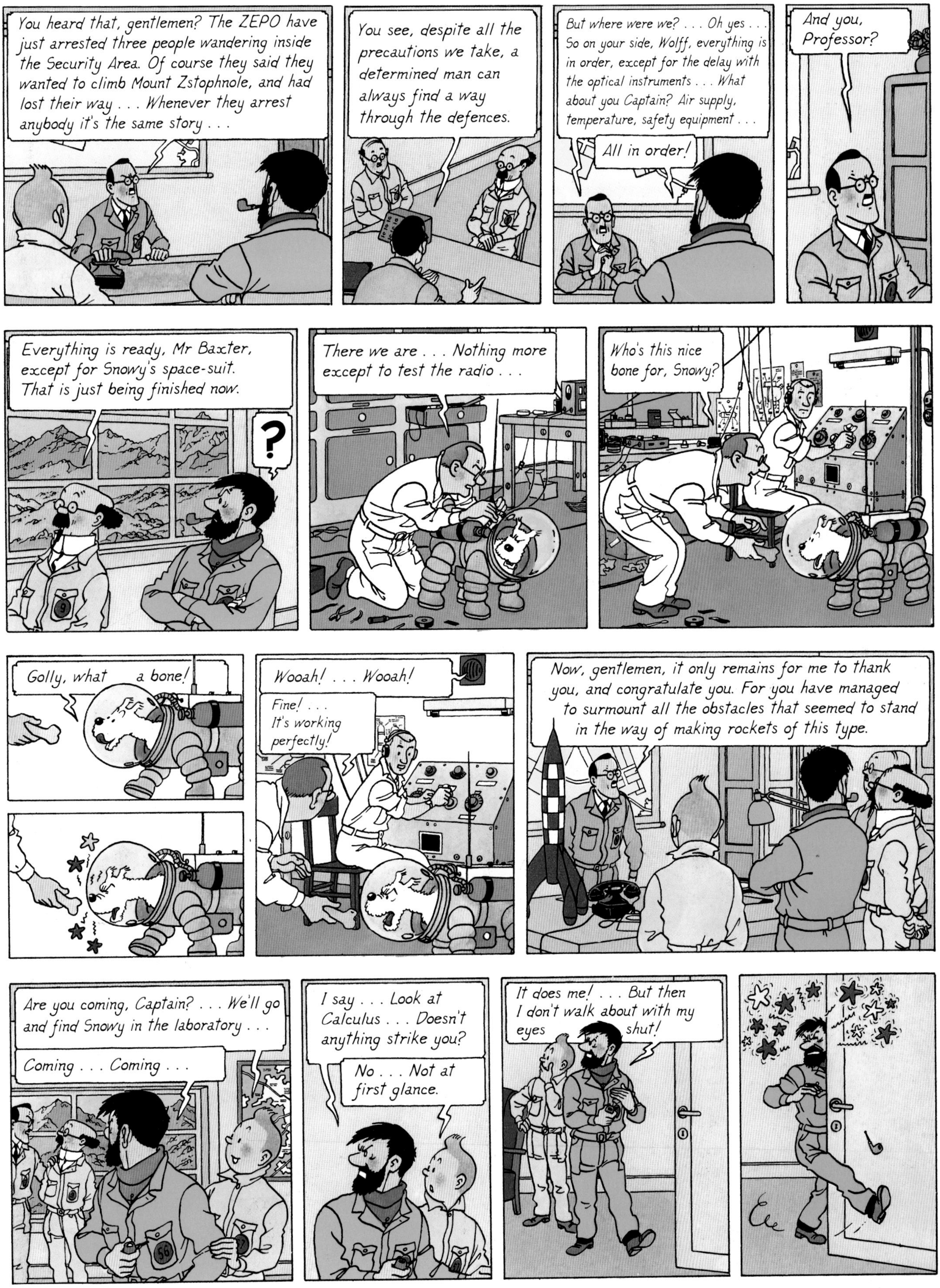

You heard that, gentlemen? The ZEPO have just arrested three people wandering inside the Security Area. Of course they said they wanted to climb Mount Zstophnole, and had lost their way . . . Whenever they arrest anybody it's the same story . . .
You see, despite all the precautions we take, a determined man can always find a way through the defences.
But where were we? . . . Oh yes . . . So on your side, Wolff, everything is in order, except for the delay with the optical instruments . . . What about you Captain? Air supply, temperature, safety equipment . . .
All in order!
And you, Professor?
Everything is ready, Mr Baxter, except for Snowy's space-suit. That is just being finished now.
?
There we are . . . Nothing more except to test the radio . . .
Who's this nice bone for, Snowy?
Golly, what a bone!
Wooah! . . . Wooah!
Fine! . . . It's working perfectly!
Now, gentlemen, it only remains for me to thank you, and congratulate you. For you have managed to surmount all the obstacles that seemed to stand in the way of making rockets of this type.
Are you coming, Captain? . . . We'll go and find Snowy in the laboratory . . .
Coming . . . Coming . . .
I say . . . Look at Calculus . . . Doesn't anything strike you?
No . . . Not at first glance.
It does me! . . . But then I don't walk about with my eyes shut!

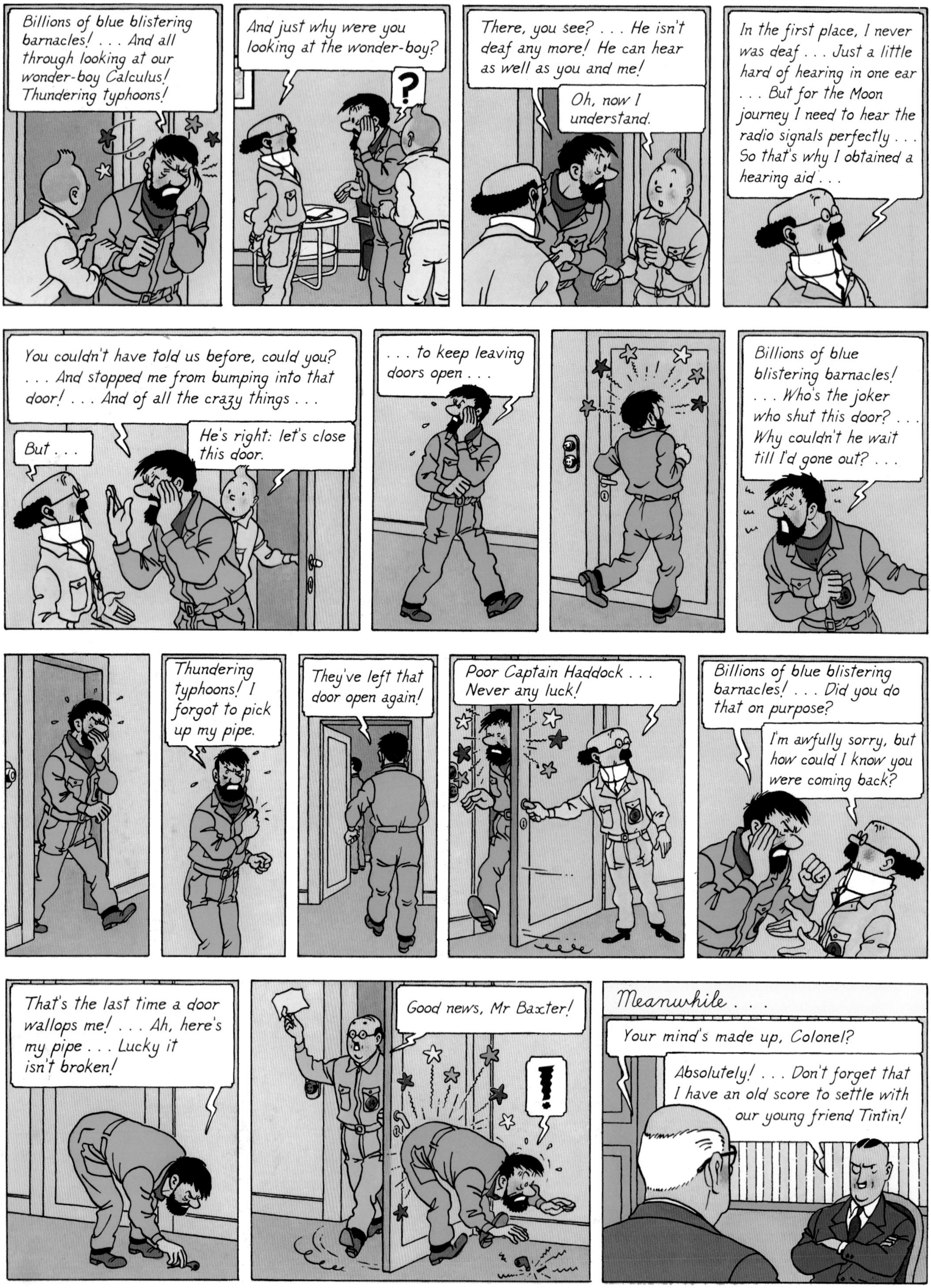

Billions of blue blistering barnacles! . . . And all through looking at our wonder-boy Calculus! Thundering typhoons!
And just why were you looking at the wonder-boy?
?
There, you see? . . . He isn't deaf any more! He can hear as well as you and me!
Oh, now I understand.
In the first place, I never was deaf . . . Just a little hard of hearing in one ear . . . But for the Moon journey I need to hear the radio signals perfectly . . . So that's why I obtained a hearing aid . . .
You couldn't have told us before, could you? . . . And stopped me from bumping into that door! . . . And of all the crazy things . . .
But . . .
He's right: let's close this door.
. . . to keep leaving doors open . . .
Billions of blue blistering barnacles! . . . Who's the joker who shut this door? . . . Why couldn't he wait till I'd gone out? . . .
Thundering typhoons! I forgot to pick up my pipe.
They've left that door open again!
Poor Captain Haddock . . . Never any luck!
Billions of blue blistering barnacles! . . . Did you do that on purpose?
I'm awfully sorry, but how could I know you were coming back?
That's the last time a door wallops me! . . . Ah, here's my pipe . . . Lucky it isn't broken!
Good news, Mr Baxter!
!
Meanwhile . . .
Your mind's made up, Colonel?
Absolutely! . . . Don't forget that I have an old score to settle with our young friend Tintin!

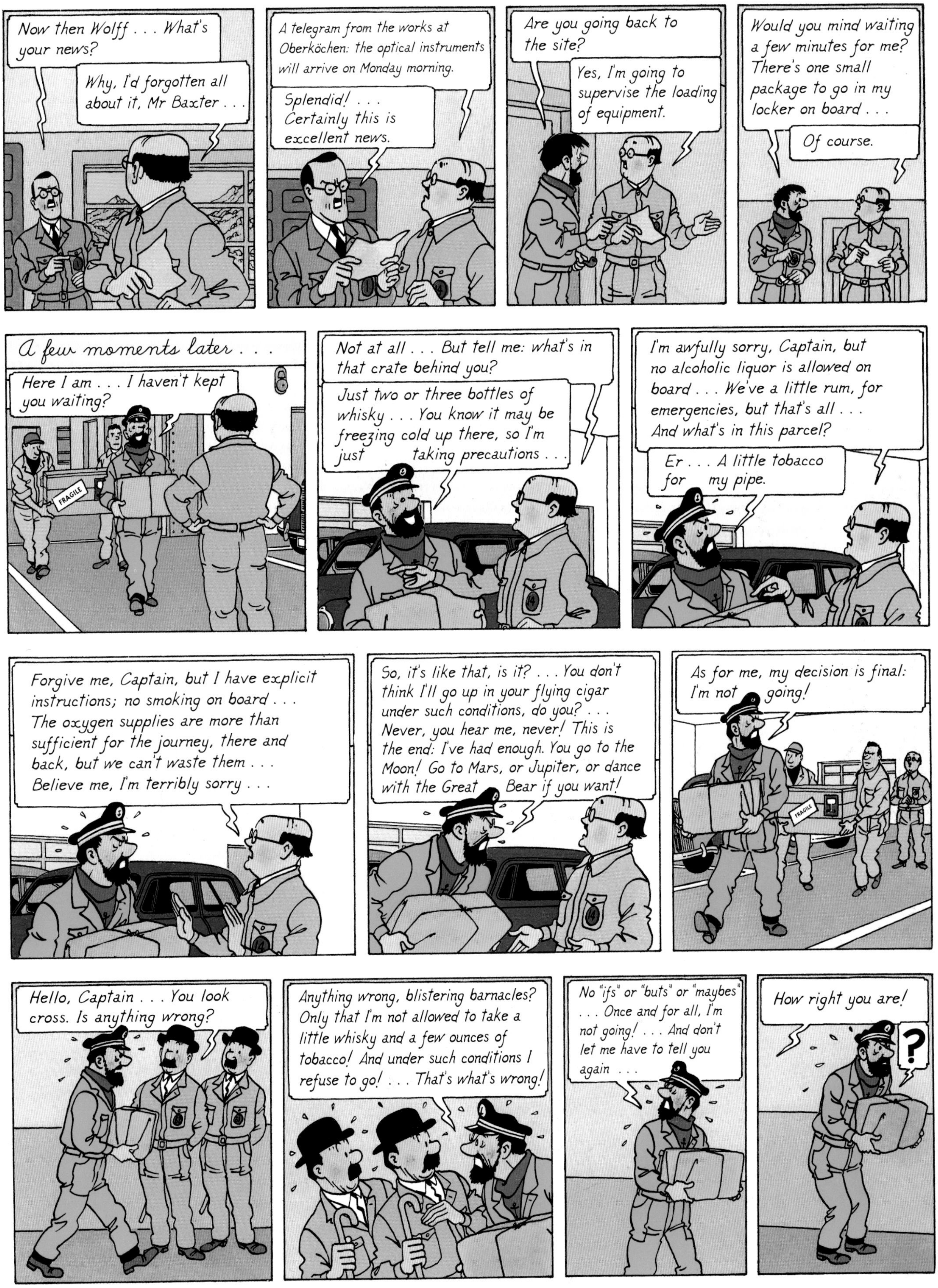

Now then Wolff . . . What's your news?
Why, I'd forgotten all about it, Mr Baxter . . .
A telegram from the works at Oberköchen: the optical instruments will arrive on Monday morning.
Splendid! . . . Certainly this is excellent news.
Are you going back to the site?
Yes, I'm going to supervise the loading of equipment.
Would you mind waiting a few minutes for me? There's one small package to go in my locker on board . . .
Of course.
A few moments later . . .
Here I am . . . I haven't kept you waiting?
FRAGILE
Not at all . . . But tell me: what's in that crate behind you?
Just two or three bottles of whisky . . . You know it may be freezing cold up there, so I'm just taking precautions . . .
I'm awfully sorry, Captain, but no alcoholic liquor is allowed on board . . . We've a little rum, for emergencies, but that's all . . . And what's in this parcel?
Er . . . A little tobacco for my pipe.
Forgive me, Captain, but I have explicit instructions; no smoking on board . . . The oxygen supplies are more than sufficient for the journey, there and back, but we can't waste them . . . Believe me, I'm terribly sorry . . .
So, it's like that, is it? . . . You don't think I'll go up in your flying cigar under such conditions, do you? . . . Never, you hear me, never! This is the end: I've had enough. You go to the Moon! Go to Mars, or Jupiter, or dance with the Great Bear if you want!
As for me, my decision is final: I'm not going!
FRAGILE
Hello, Captain . . . You look cross. Is anything wrong?
Anything wrong, blistering barnacles? Only that I'm not allowed to take a little whisky and a few ounces of tobacco! And under such conditions I refuse to go! . . . That's what's wrong!
No "ifs" or "buts" or "maybes" . . . Once and for all, I'm not going! . . . And don't let me have to tell you again . . .
How right you are!
?

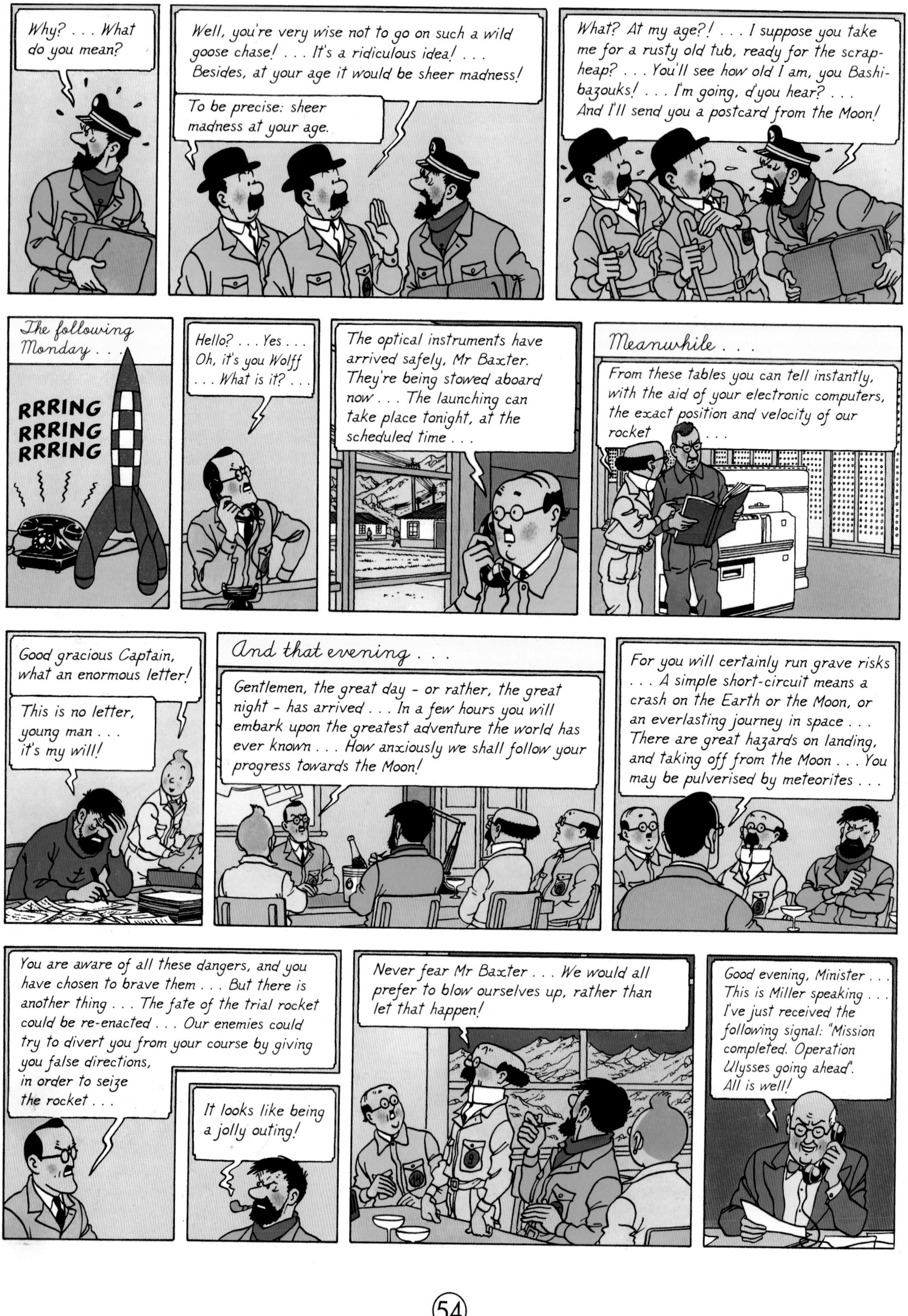

Why? . . . What do you mean?
Well, you're very wise not to go on such a wild goose chase! . . . It's a ridiculous idea! . . . Besides, at your age it would be sheer madness!
To be precise: sheer madness at your age.
What? At my age?! . . . I suppose you take me for a rusty old tub, ready for the scrap-heap? . . . You'll see how old I am, you Bashi-bazouks! . . . I'm going, d'you hear? . . . And I'll send you a postcard from the Moon!
The following Monday . . .
RRRING RRRING RRRING
Hello? . . . Yes . . . Oh, it's you Wolff . . . What is it? . . .
The optical instruments have arrived safely, Mr Baxter. They're being stowed aboard now . . . The launching can take place tonight, at the scheduled time . . .
Meanwhile . . .
From these tables you can tell instantly, with the aid of your electronic computers, the exact position and velocity of our rocket . . .
Good gracious Captain, what an enormous letter!
This is no letter, young man . . . it's my will!
And that evening . . .
Gentlemen, the great day - or rather, the great night - has arrived . . . In a few hours you will embark upon the greatest adventure the world has ever known . . . How anxiously we shall follow your progress towards the Moon!
For you will certainly run grave risks . . . A simple short-circuit means a crash on the Earth or the Moon, or an everlasting journey in space . . . There are great hazards on landing, and taking off from the Moon . . . You may be pulverised by meteorites . . .
You are aware of all these dangers, and you have chosen to brave them . . . But there is another thing . . . The fate of the trial rocket could be re-enacted . . . Our enemies could try to divert you from your course by giving you false directions, in order to seize the rocket . . .
It looks like being a jolly outing!
Never fear Mr Baxter . . . We would all prefer to blow ourselves up, rather than let that happen!
Good evening, Minister . . . This is Miller speaking . . . I've just received the following signal: "Mission completed. Operation Ulysses going ahead". All is well!

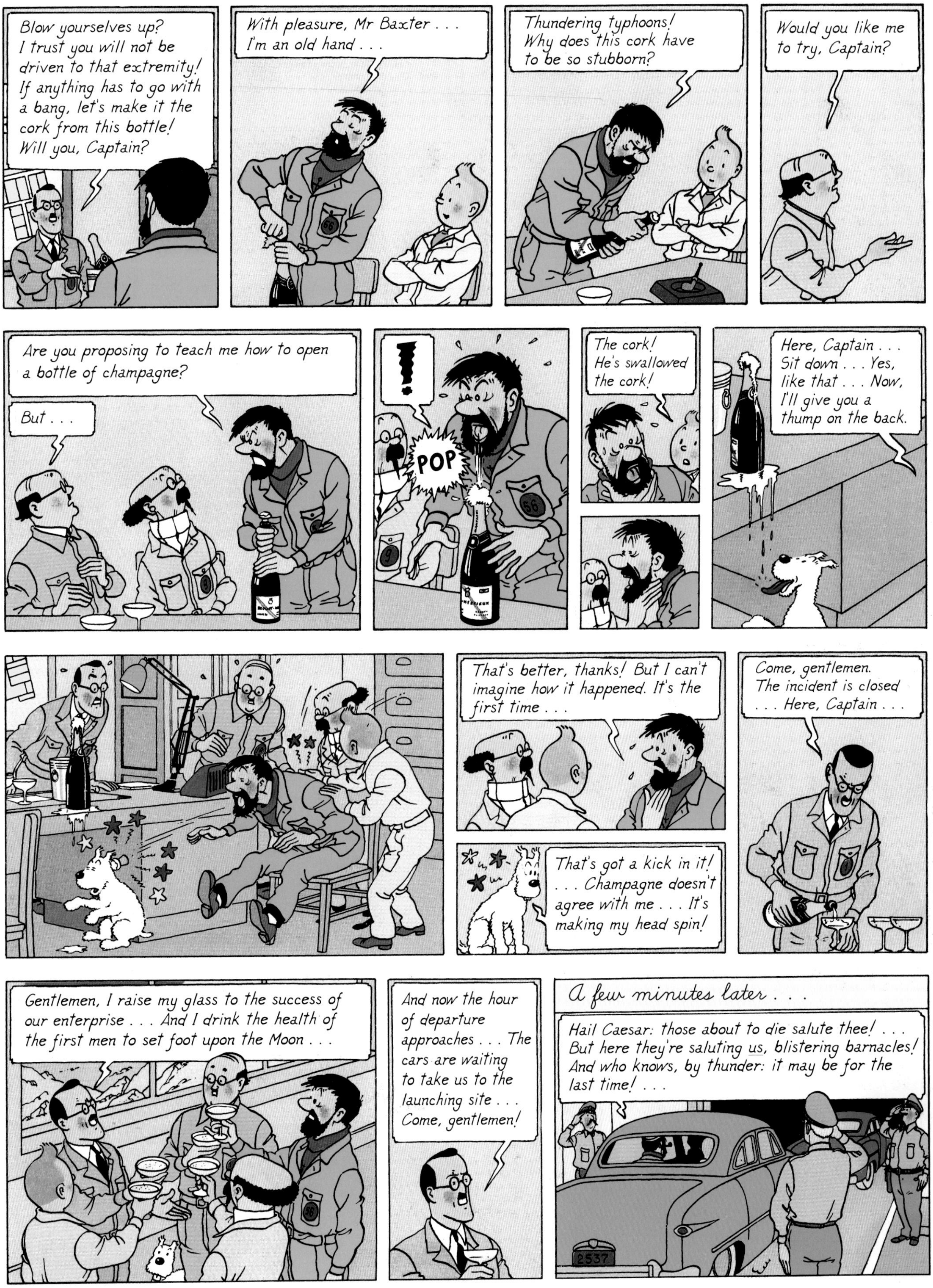
Blow yourselves up? I trust you will not be driven to that extremity! If anything has to go with a bang, let's make it the cork from this bottle! Will you, Captain?
With pleasure, Mr Baxter . . . I'm an old hand . . .
Thundering typhoons! Why does this cork have to be so stubborn?
Would you like me to try, Captain?
Are you proposing to teach me how to open a bottle of champagne?
But . . .
!
POP
The cork! He's swallowed the cork!
Here, Captain . . . Sit down . . . Yes, like that . . . Now, I'll give you a thump on the back.
That's better, thanks! But I can't imagine how it happened. It's the first time . . .
That's got a kick in it! . . . Champagne doesn't agree with me . . . It's making my head spin!
Come, gentlemen. The incident is closed . . . Here, Captain . . .
Gentlemen, I raise my glass to the success of our enterprise . . . And I drink the health of the first men to set foot upon the Moon . . .
And now the hour of departure approaches . . . The cars are waiting to take us to the launching site . . . Come, gentlemen!
A few minutes later . . .
Hail Caesar: those about to die salute thee! . . . But here they're saluting us, blistering barnacles! And who knows, by thunder: it may be for the last time! . . .
2537

I must say you don't look very happy, Captain.

Why on earth should I look happy? Because we're off to the Moon?

To the Moon! . . . Don't make me laugh! . . . If that honky-tonk Calculus-machine doesn't blow up at the start, we'll find ourselves roaming around between the Great Bear and Jupiter, and never come back! You can hoot with laughter about that if you   like!

No, I meant . . . Oh look, Captain! We're there!

Look! The gantries are floodlit; the rocket is ready for launching! It's like magic!

Yes, very pretty . . . for the spectators! . . .

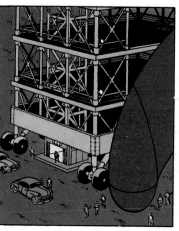

So there's the machine to which we're entrusting our lives! . . . It's sheer lunacy! . . . Just think: through me Calculus recovered his memory, and completed this crazy scheme! I'll never forgive myself!

Meanwhile . . .

If there's no change of plan, it's just half an hour till their departure . . .

56

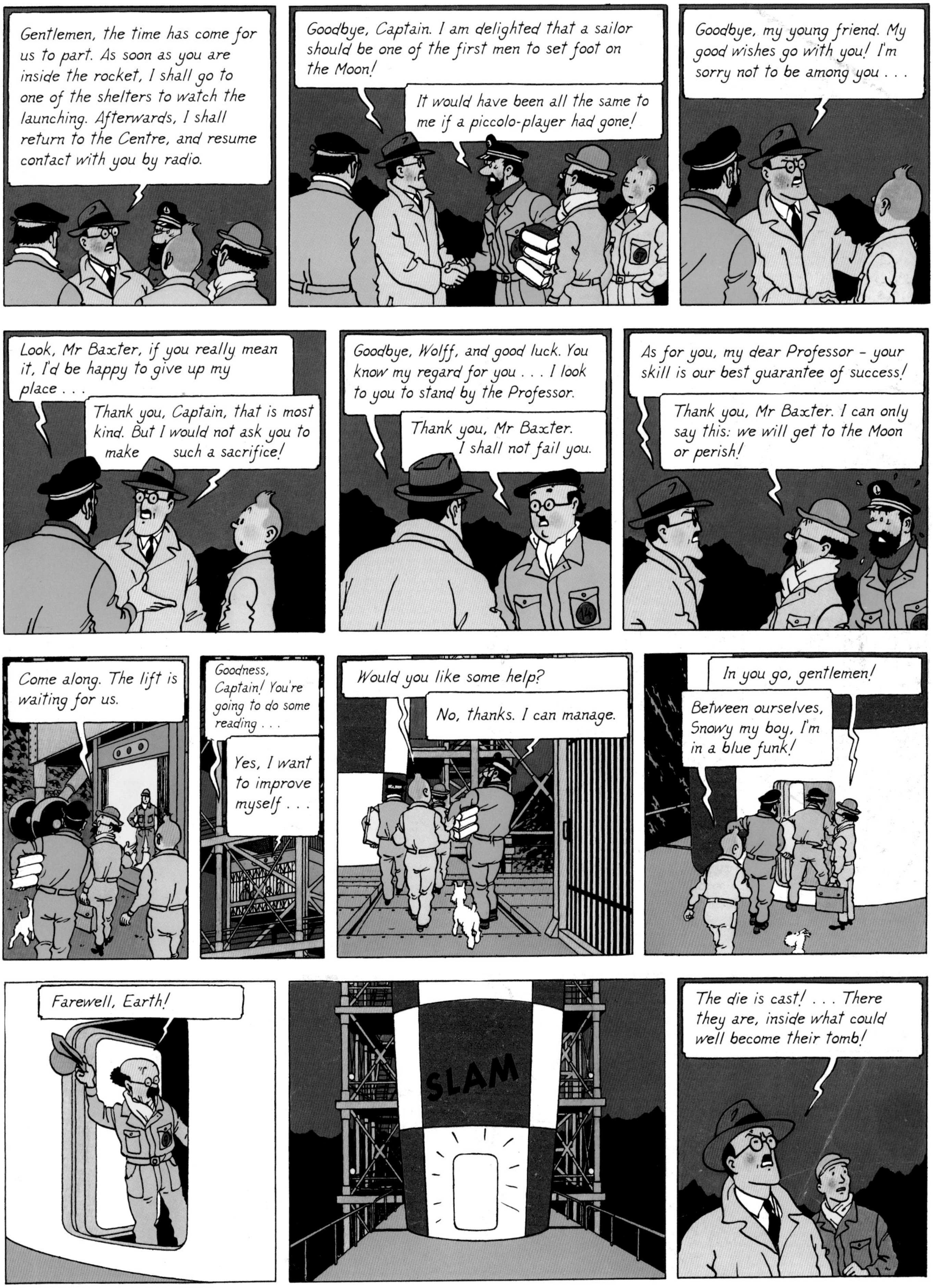

Gentlemen, the time has come for us to part. As soon as you are inside the rocket, I shall go to one of the shelters to watch the launching. Afterwards, I shall return to the Centre, and resume contact with you by radio.
Goodbye, Captain. I am delighted that a sailor should be one of the first men to set foot on the Moon!
It would have been all the same to me if a piccolo-player had gone!
Goodbye, my young friend. My good wishes go with you! I'm sorry not to be among you . . .
Look, Mr Baxter, if you really mean it, I'd be happy to give up my place . . .
Thank you, Captain, that is most kind. But I would not ask you to make such a sacrifice!
Goodbye, Wolff, and good luck. You know my regard for you . . . I look to you to stand by the Professor.
Thank you, Mr Baxter. I shall not fail you.
As for you, my dear Professor – your skill is our best guarantee of success!
Thank you, Mr Baxter. I can only say this: we will get to the Moon or perish!
Come along. The lift is waiting for us.
Goodness, Captain! You're going to do some reading . . .
Yes, I want to improve myself . . .
Would you like some help?
No, thanks. I can manage.
In you go, gentlemen!
Between ourselves, Snowy my boy, I'm in a blue funk!
Farewell, Earth!
SLAM
The die is cast! . . . There they are, inside what could well become their tomb!

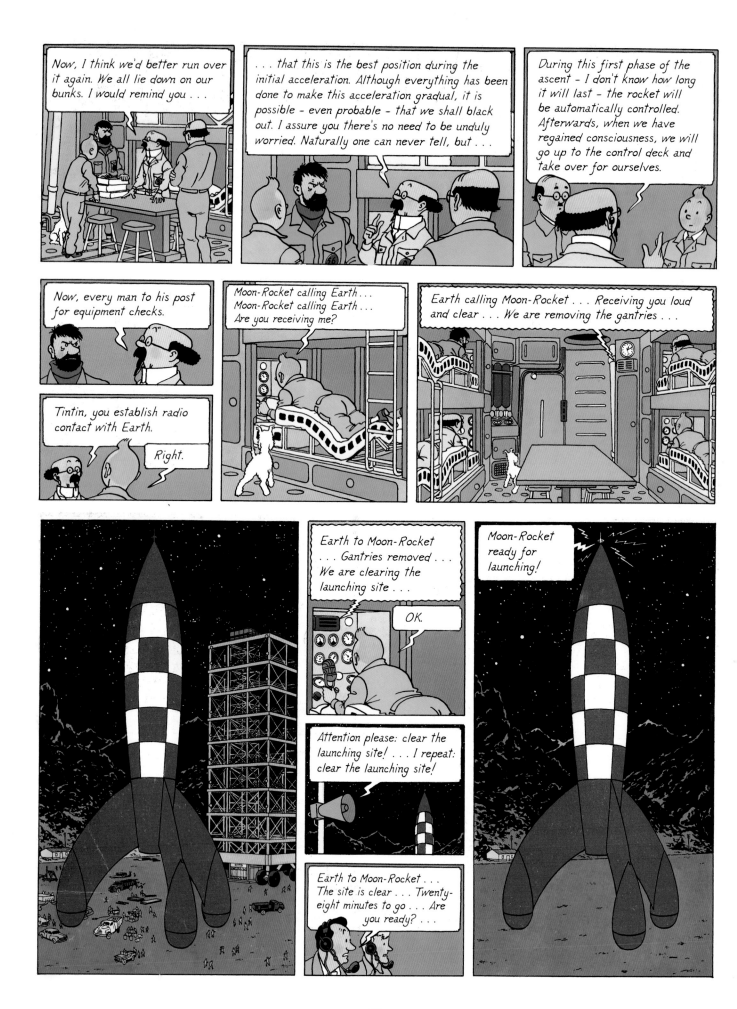

Now, I think we'd better run over it again. We all lie down on our bunks. I would remind you . . .

. . . that this is the best position during the initial acceleration. Although everything has been done to make this acceleration gradual, it is possible - even probable - that we shall black out. I assure you there's no need to be unduly worried. Naturally one can never tell, but . . .

During this first phase of the ascent - I don't know how long it will last - the rocket will be automatically controlled. Afterwards, when we have regained consciousness, we will go up to the control deck and take over for ourselves.

Now, every man to his post for equipment checks.

Tintin, you establish radio contact with Earth.

Right.

Moon-Rocket calling Earth . . . Moon-Rocket calling Earth . . . Are you receiving me?

Earth calling Moon-Rocket . . . Receiving you loud and clear . . . We are removing the gantries . . .

Earth to Moon-Rocket . . . Gantries removed . . . We are clearing the launching site . . .

OK.

Moon-Rocket ready for launching!

Attention please: clear the launching site! . . . I repeat: clear the launching site!

Earth to Moon-Rocket . . . The site is clear . . . Twenty-eight minutes to go . . . Are you ready? . . .

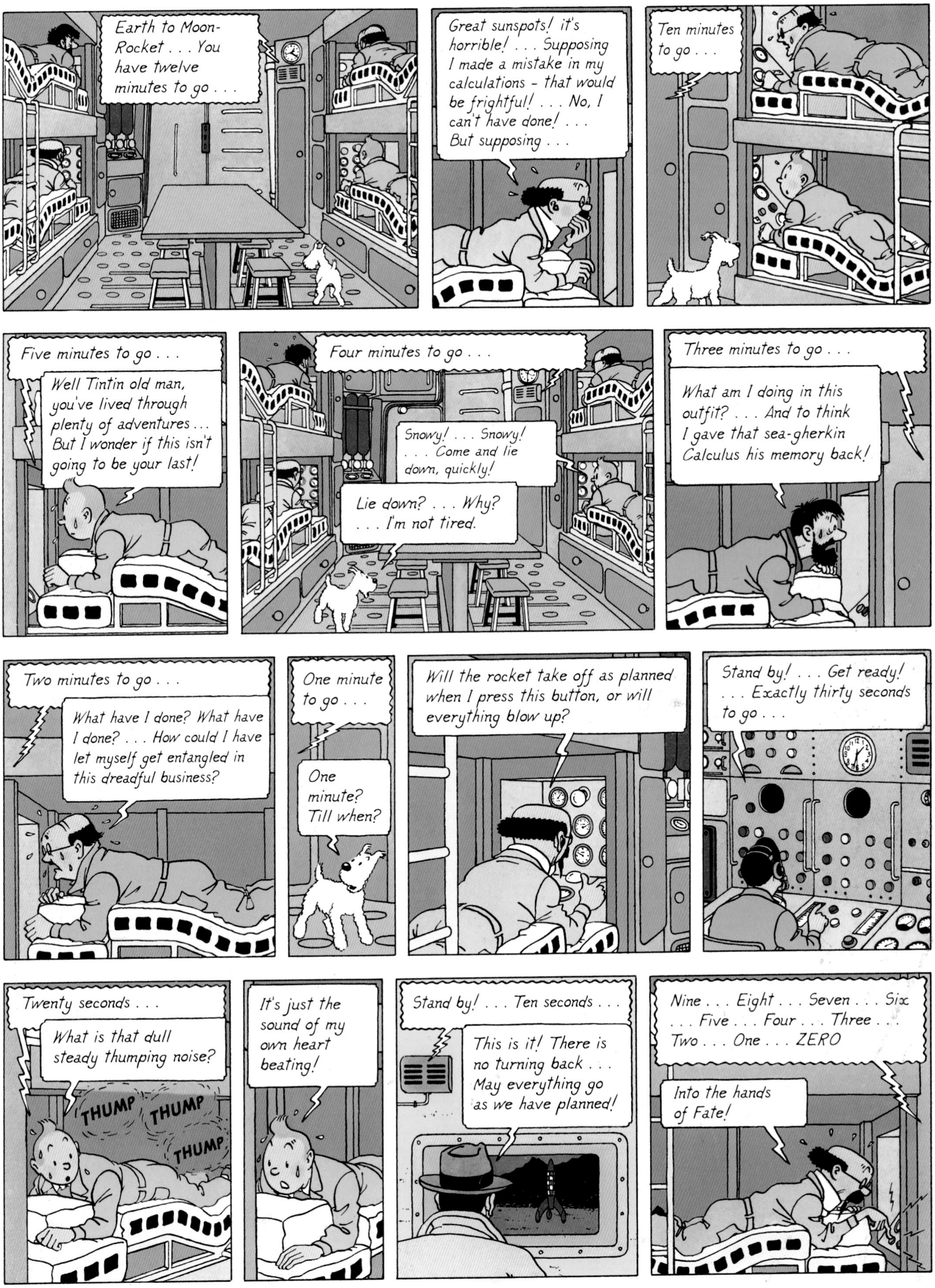
Earth to Moon-Rocket . . . You have twelve minutes to go . . .
Great sunspots! it's horrible! . . . Supposing I made a mistake in my calculations - that would be frightful! . . . No, I can't have done! . . . But supposing . . .
Ten minutes to go . . .
Five minutes to go . . .
Well Tintin old man, you've lived through plenty of adventures . . . But I wonder if this isn't going to be your last!
Four minutes to go . . .
Snowy! . . . Snowy! . . . Come and lie down, quickly!
Lie down? . . . Why? . . . I'm not tired.
Three minutes to go . . .
What am I doing in this outfit? . . . And to think I gave that sea-gherkin Calculus his memory back!
Two minutes to go . . .
What have I done? What have I done? . . . How could I have let myself get entangled in this dreadful business?
One minute to go . . .
One minute? Till when?
Will the rocket take off as planned when I press this button, or will everything blow up?
Stand by! . . . Get ready! . . . Exactly thirty seconds to go . . .
Twenty seconds . . .
What is that dull steady thumping noise?
THUMP THUMP THUMP
It's just the sound of my own heart beating!
Stand by! . . . Ten seconds . . .
This is it! There is no turning back . . . May everything go as we have planned!
Nine . . . Eight . . . Seven . . . Six . . . Five . . . Four . . . Three . . . Two . . . One . . . ZERO
Into the hands of Fate!

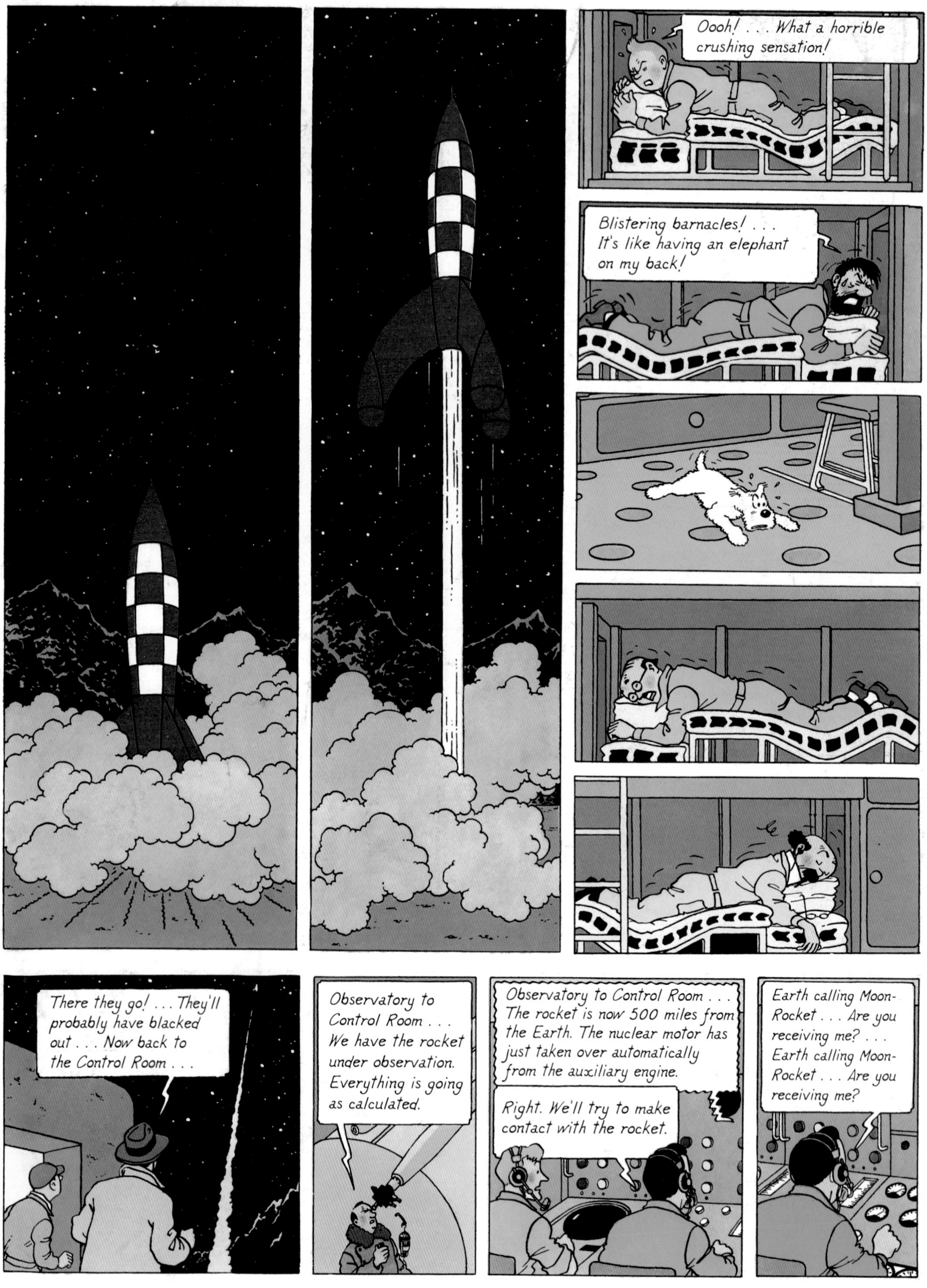

Oooh! . . . What a horrible crushing sensation!
Blistering barnacles! . . . It's like having an elephant on my back!
There they go! . . . They'll probably have blacked out . . . Now back to the Control Room . . .
Observatory to Control Room . . . We have the rocket under observation. Everything is going as calculated.
Observatory to Control Room . . . The rocket is now 500 miles from the Earth. The nuclear motor has just taken over automatically from the auxiliary engine.
Right. We'll try to make contact with the rocket.
Earth calling Moon-Rocket . . . Are you receiving me? . . . Earth calling Moon-Rocket . . . Are you receiving me?

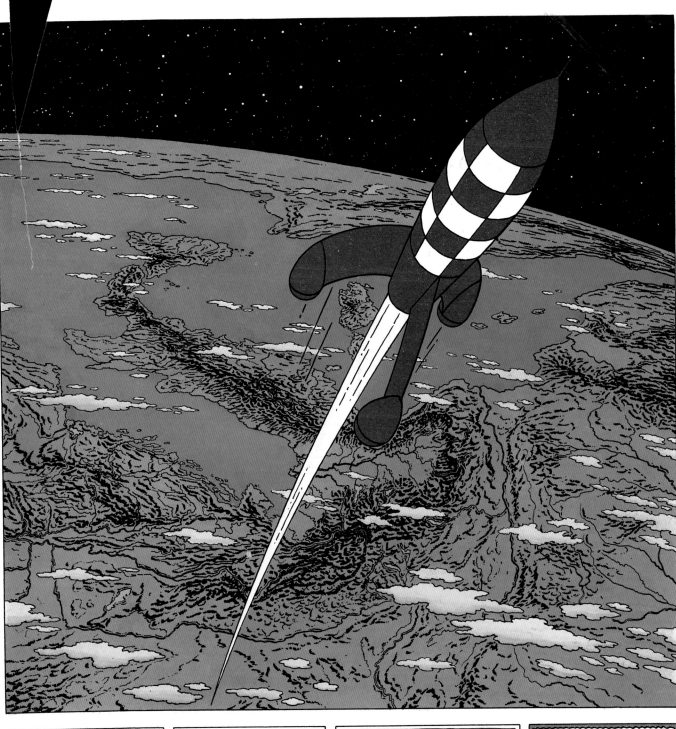

Earth calling Moon-Rocket . . . Are you receiving me? . . . Are you receiving me? . . .

Observatory to Control Room . . . The rocket's altitude is now 1000 miles. Have you succeeded in establishing radio contact yet? Please report . . .

Earth calling Moon-Rocket . . . Are you receiving me? . . . Earth calling Moon-Rocket . . .

Control Room to Observatory . . . The Moon-Rocket is not answering.

Earth calling Moon-Rocket . . . Are you receiving me? . . . Earth calling . . .

By Lucifer! Surely nothing can have gone wrong?

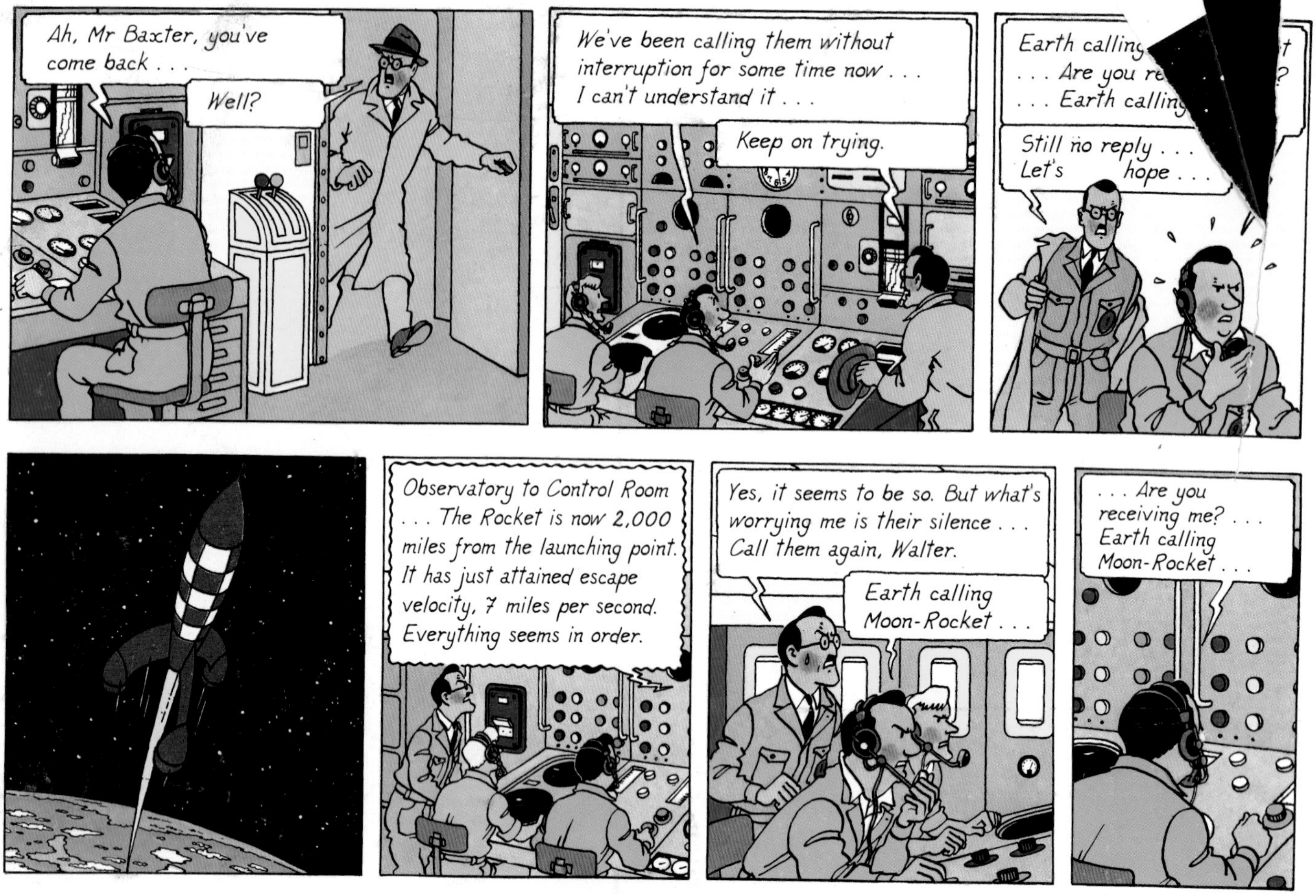
Ah, Mr Baxter, you've come back . . .
Well?
We've been calling them without interruption for some time now . . . I can't understand it . . .
Keep on trying.
Earth calling
. . . Are you re
. . . Earth calling
Still no reply . . . Let's hope . . .
Observatory to Control Room . . . The Rocket is now 2,000 miles from the launching point. It has just attained escape velocity, 7 miles per second. Everything seems in order.
Yes, it seems to be so. But what's worrying me is their silence . . . Call them again, Walter.
Earth calling Moon-Rocket . . .
. . . Are you receiving me? . . . Earth calling Moon-Rocket . . .

What dangers await Tintin and his friends on the Moon?

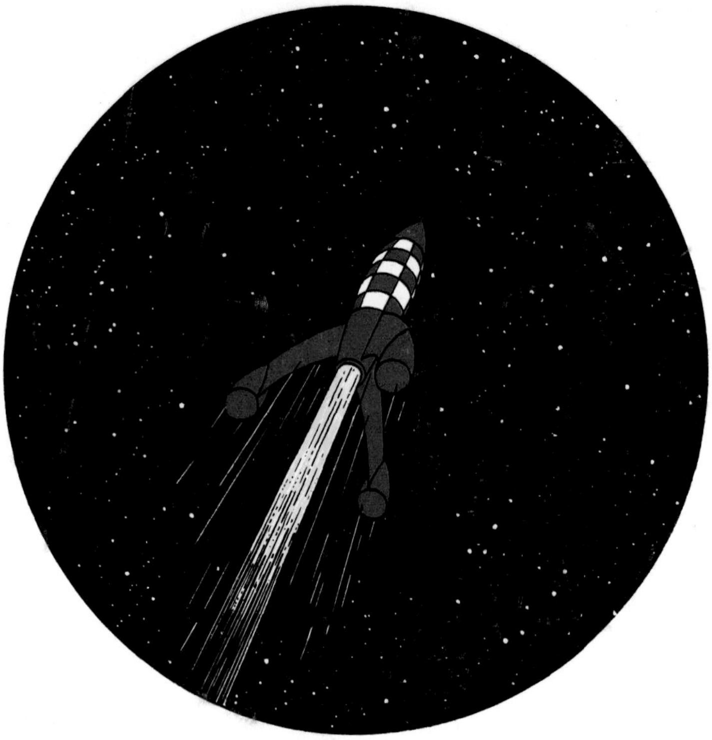

What will happen on this perilous journey into space?

Will they ever return to Earth? You can join in the rest of their great adventure when you read

EXPLORERS ON THE MOON